## Bolan had a grim idea of what he would find

Anger pumped in rhythm to the beating of his heart. Sobbing and soft voices reached his ears, followed by gruff demands for silence. Then he heard Katerina Muscovky quietly calling to him as he struggled to sit up. The real world of hooded gunmen and hostages came into slow focus.

His first thought was to free himself and strike back. How to do that was a damn good question that presented no ready answers. The others might have been clinging to some faint hope of rescue or release, but Bolan knew from experience what their captors were capable of doing.

Looking at the cameras on tripods, he knew he'd better find a solution fast—before the filmed executions began.

# MACK BOLAN ®

## The Executioner

| | |
|---|---|
| #256 Point of Impact | #294 Scorpion Rising |
| #257 Precision Play | #295 Hostile Alliance |
| #258 Target Lock | #296 Nuclear Game |
| #259 Nightfire | #297 Deadly Pursuit |
| #260 Dayhunt | #298 Final Play |
| #261 Dawnkill | #299 Dangerous Encounter |
| #262 Trigger Point | #300 Warrior's Requiem |
| #263 Skysniper | #301 Blast Radius |
| #264 Iron Fist | #302 Shadow Search |
| #265 Freedom Force | #303 Sea of Terror |
| #266 Ultimate Price | #304 Soviet Specter |
| #267 Invisible Invader | #305 Point Position |
| #268 Shattered Trust | #306 Mercy Mission |
| #269 Shifting Shadows | #307 Hard Pursuit |
| #270 Judgment Day | #308 Into the Fire |
| #271 Cyberhunt | #309 Flames of Fury |
| #272 Stealth Striker | #310 Killing Heat |
| #273 UForce | #311 Night of the Knives |
| #274 Rogue Target | #312 Death Gamble |
| #275 Crossed Borders | #313 Lockdown |
| #276 Leviathan | #314 Lethal Payload |
| #277 Dirty Mission | #315 Agent of Peril |
| #278 Triple Reverse | #316 Poison Justice |
| #279 Fire Wind | #317 Hour of Judgment |
| #280 Fear Rally | #318 Code of Resistance |
| #281 Blood Stone | #319 Entry Point |
| #282 Jungle Conflict | #320 Exit Code |
| #283 Ring of Retaliation | #321 Suicide Highway |
| #284 Devil's Army | #322 Time Bomb |
| #285 Final Strike | #323 Soft Target |
| #286 Armageddon Exit | #324 Terminal Zone |
| #287 Rogue Warrior | #325 Edge of Hell |
| #288 Arctic Blast | #326 Blood Tide |
| #289 Vendetta Force | #327 Serpent's Lair |
| #290 Pursued | #328 Triangle of Terror |
| #291 Blood Trade | #329 Hostile Crossing |
| #292 Savage Game | #330 Dual Action |
| #293 Death Merchants | #331 Assault Force |

# The Don Pendleton's Executioner®

## ASSAULT FORCE

### A GOLD EAGLE BOOK FROM

# WORLDWIDE®

TORONTO • NEW YORK • LONDON
AMSTERDAM • PARIS • SYDNEY • HAMBURG
STOCKHOLM • ATHENS • TOKYO • MILAN
MADRID • WARSAW • BUDAPEST • AUCKLAND

First edition June 2006
ISBN 0-373-64331-4

Special thanks and acknowledgment to
Dan Schmidt for his contribution to this work.

ASSAULT FORCE

**Printed in U.S.A.**

Heroes as great have died, and yet shall fall.
—Homer, c1000 B.C.
*Iliad*

Big screen heroes are larger than life. Real-life heroes often go unnoticed.
—Mack Bolan

# THE
## MACK BOLAN
### LEGEND

Nothing less than a war could have fashioned the destiny of the man called Mack Bolan. Bolan earned the Executioner title in the jungle hell of Vietnam.

But this soldier also wore another name—Sergeant Mercy. He was so tagged because of the compassion he showed to wounded comrades-in-arms and Vietnamese civilians.

Mack Bolan's second tour of duty ended prematurely when he was given emergency leave to return home and bury his family, victims of the Mob. Then he declared a one-man war against the Mafia.

He confronted the Families head-on from coast to coast, and soon a hope of victory began to appear. But Bolan had broken society's every rule. That same society started gunning for this elusive warrior—to no avail.

So Bolan was offered amnesty to work within the system against terrorism. This time, as an employee of Uncle Sam, Bolan became Colonel John Phoenix. With a command center at Stony Man Farm in Virginia, he and his new allies—Able Team and Phoenix Force—waged relentless war on a new adversary: the KGB.

But when his one true love, April Rose, died at the hands of the Soviet terror machine, Bolan severed all ties with Establishment authority.

Now, after a lengthy lone-wolf struggle and much soul-searching, the Executioner has agreed to enter an "arm's-length" alliance with his government once more, reserving the right to pursue personal missions in his Everlasting War.

**1**

He stepped onto the wide, white-marbled path, leaving the revelry of the withering beach crowd behind as shadows lengthened across the Mediterranean. The sound of the gentle lap of waves faded the deeper he forged into the army of guests and locals marching for the bars, restaurants and discos. He considered—despite some anticipated alteration in professional standards—that he was still in a class all by himself. Come what may, he was nothing less than a superman in black ops, the Entity, to be more precise, as he so often thought of himself. He was above the laws of man and whatever gods they worshiped. Fear God? Respect Man? Perish the absurd thought.

Beyond professional pride and infinite confidence in his own lethal skills, he knew his continued existence depended on his ability to remain a nameless, faceless specter. Positive identification, after all, could mean sudden death.

Which was why he never left whatever his lair of the moment without some bogus credentials. Depending on the situation, he was FBI Special Agent Henry Jarrod, Pierre DeJaureaux of Interpol or at present, Jarrod Harmon, head of security for the American Embassy in Spain, which in special ops and intelligence circles translated CIA. A chameleon walking a tightrope, for damn sure, he never moved among prey or predators without the 9 mm Browning Hi-Power stowed in shoulder rigging.

He took his time strolling up the low incline, apparently sightseeing, but grimly aware the clock was winding down for the big event. The roving traffic, he noted with keen fondness, was mostly stunning females, two, maybe three beauties per man. European, African or Asian, it was a rainbow of nubile flesh, begging to be devoured, barely concealed in sheer wrap-arounds for cocktail hour, a thong bikini, here and there, to really get his pulse pounding. Feeling invincible in his own tanned war hide, hefting the heavy nylon duffel bag, he dismissed the men as standard nonthreatening Eurotrash with more money than spine. He let his eyes fill behind the mirrored shades with fleeting fantasies of women in the prayer position. And who knew? he thought, when the time came...

Hell, when it began they would hit their knees, all of them, make no mistake.

Business first, he told himself, and felt his lust spiral down toward a dark pit of churning anger and resentment as he heard women giggle over the spray and hiss of fountains, hidden as they were in private cubbyholes off to the sides in this tunnel of transplanted jungle Eden. Still, the heavenly fragrance of all this sun-bronzed perfumed cream and hairspray was a heady mix in his nose. It seemed to swell the air, drawing him, in fact, toward destiny as he closed on a pool near football field dimensions—a watery playground with all the posh trimmings of fountains, palm trees, custom hot tubs, with scores of buxom bunnies in skintight one-pieces clacking along on high heels to keep the drinks flowing.

Let the good times roll.

Heaven was soon to be set on fire.

A check of his Rolex watch indicated he was minutes late

after shoring up eleventh-hour details. But the man would keep, if he was as brazen and committed as his track record declared, and wished to see his own dream come true.

Harmon had no doubt on those two fronts, but seeing was still believing in his playbook.

A trio of leggy blondes swept past, the aroma of sweet candy flesh nearly knocking him out of his Italian loafers. Enough. Get laser-focused on mission parameters, he warned himself. He was about to nail down all the fine details with a sorcerer's touch. He wasn't any playboy here to grab ass, at least not in the foreseeable future.

Topping the rise, Jarrod Harmon marched onto the concrete decking and smiled despite his best intentions. Giant palmettos fanned away on both sides, more man-made jungle. There were cabanas, poolside bars with thatched roofs, pockets of marble tables around the deck. Chaise lounges and leather chairs became thrones for the elite, erect and proud all of them, modern-day kings and queens, not a care in the world.

He suddenly felt his mood darken, lost the smile as the enormity of the mission slammed like a meteor on his shoulders. He froze in midstride, the clamor of joy and freedom, the smell of arrogant money and rich, sated flesh was like a living barrier falling over him.

Everywhere they were laughing, hyenas in human skin, a babble of tongues raised in grand spirits from the dozen or so dialects of Spain and other countries. They clinked glasses, kissed, embraced, downing one drink after another like there was no tomorrow—and, oh, if they only knew, he thought. They frolicked in the water, splashing around like innocent children. A pair of ripe melons flashed for his eyes to behold as some joker held up a bikini top like a trophy.

Soft music piped in from invisible amplifiers, a melodious

love song, it sounded, as if the flames of lust really needed stoking. So much jewelry glinting in the sunshine, it was like watching countless stars wink wherever he turned, a sea of wealth flaunted to signal the peasants to stand back, gape and wish.

All the beautiful people.

He realized just how different he was from them, but also how much he hated them. None of them could even begin to fathom the dark, angry, bloody world from which he came, had probably never known a tough day in their lives. Their existence was a gilded, privileged fortress, a towering wall, a great chasm that kept him...

Oh, but how sweet it would be.

Another panning scour and he detailed the security guards, staggered at intervals on both sides of the pool. Six in all, easy enough to spot, they were little more than clones in black jackets, dark shades and earplugs, muscle attempting to look casual but failing. Sacrificial idiots.

Harmon stared at the palatial monument where it would all happen.

Twelve stories, he considered, 683 rooms. More than three miles of corridors, and capacity enough for close to five thousand bodies. The ritzy nirvana for the rich and famous was purgatory for service staff, a small city unto itself. A multibillion dollar facelift was on the drawing board to stretch even farther up the coast, he knew. Those dream teams of architects and engineers—backed by private Saudi cash—were still hard at it to pick clean every last sore of the old barrios, upgrade marinas to berth seven-figure yachts and flashy cigarette boats.

The New Barcelona Hotel.

Staring at the top floor of Presidential Suites, he tried to envision the interior layout from memory, but already knew he'd fall short. Between ballrooms and dining rooms, restaurants, bars and clubs, the shopping complex, the spas and gymnasium…throw in cinemas, the vast expanse of kitchen with staff that rolled out entrées, buffets and room service meals around-the-clock, the security-management-utility vault belowground…

How in the world were they going to pull it off? he wondered.

Nothing but a challenge, he told himself, the biggest to date, without question, but he was, after all, the Entity.

He rolled on, shouldered past some guy in nut huggers, sending his umbrella drink airborne. The squawk of French outrage was music to his ears as he set his sights on the hoopla at the pavilion on the north edge. The gold lion on its haunches, all of two stories and maybe thirty feet across with shamelessly displayed testicles the size of small cars, was his signpost. As he drew closer to the gaggle of reporters and autograph hounds—mostly teenaged kids, a smattering of female oglers—Harmon couldn't help but indulge a wide smile, nurse some contempt.

America's new celluloid action hero and the hottest matinee idol in Europe was in town to scout locations for his latest flick. Harmon had seen the guy's mug and muscled self—always grim and wielding guns the size of howitzers—plastered all over the place during the dry run. Half of six in-house screens were running the drivel daily. Little did big shot know, Harmon thought, he and his entourage had made the cut, all destined for stardom in a script already written and approved.

Marching toward the gilded lion, Harmon suddenly felt worlds collide. It happened sometimes when driven toward a fate so bold. Armored with little more than experience, guts and sense of utter invincibility, sight and sound meshed, a living vacuum, it felt, sucking him toward destiny even as physical reality ground into slow motion. Human beings? Scapegoats? Sacrificial lambs? Look at them, he thought. They were oblivious, the walking dead, shielded in privilege and money, above it all.

He felt their energy, drawing it into the fire igniting inside. He became so acutely aware of his own lethal uniqueness it was as if he was floating past the group by the statue. The King of Tinseltown, he observed in the shining haze of his adrenalized free-floating state, fit the bill, as far as standard film handsome went. Tall, broad, dark-haired, the six-figure pearly whites flashed at the adoring throngs. A leggy, large-breasted bimbo adorned each muscled arm. With black shades hiding action hero's eyes, Harmon couldn't get a read into the man's soul as he passed before the gold lion, angling for the bar set beneath the marble rooftop.

But he could read the type. Two gorillas were on standby, scowling unchained beasts, set to slap anyone who got out of line with the movie star or didn't pay sufficient homage. The man was early thirty-something, but Harmon believed he could absorb the star's life force easily enough. He marked him as a pampered, overindulged phony who would most likely curl up into a fetal position at the first sign of real danger—just another Hollywood asshole.

The entourage staking out tables beside the film hero was an interesting mix, however. The usual squeeze things, of course, there to keep the star happy. A trio of jokers stuffed into four-figure suits looked properly self-important, directors or whatever else, women hanging on their every breath. A few scruffy, bleary-eyed guys down the line, minus the chicks, looked as harried as hell, hard-core boozers the way they hit the drinks. Harmon read them as being forever worried about job security as they rifled through papers, all animated heated talk. He figured scriptwriters, the unsung fuel that powered any Hollywood juggernaut. One guy, who might have been a ringer for the star—or close enough at first look—sat with two men. The physical double of the star, only light-years tougher, Harmon chalked him up as ex-military. All of them were clearly unimpressed with the showboating. They were confident and comfortable in their skin as only men who'd been down some dark alleys and walked out standing could be. Had to be stuntmen, the real deal, taking all the risks while getting slapped around and abused, humiliated and killed for the greater glory of the hero. Bunch of damn nonsense. For his money, judging them as nothing less than solid balls-to-the-wall stand-up acts, the roles should have been reversed.

Only in Hollywood.

Choking down a raw smart-ass one-liner, satisfied to reserve it, nonetheless, Harmon hastened his strides. He was past the empty bandstand, unattended instruments waiting to woo the happy-hour crowd, when he spotted his man. Harmon fell into his meandering guest act next, smiling at the milling crowd, inhaling the rich aroma of the best food money could buy as waiters in black tuxedos set up the buffet. The bar was packed tight with suits and skirts, but the high leather chair was empty next to his man, as he had known it would be. There was enough barfly tumult for their purposes. He glanced at the swarthy handsome face bent over a bottle of beer. Smiling, he said, "Is this seat taken, sir?"

Without looking up, the slightly built dark man answered back in Castilian Spanish, "It's reserved for you."

Harmon settled in, dumped the bag on the deck, managed to catch the bartender on the fly and ordered a beer with a whiskey chaser. Then he looked around, smiling, awed by it all. He sensed before seeing him, the man's backup at the far end of the bar. He had no names, had never met them, but he knew the look of a killer when he saw it. He spotted a couple of his own guys in a booth to his deep four o'clock. Lighting a cigarette, Harmon rode out the silence while the bartender fetched his order. Cool was important, deceptive appearances critical in case unwanted eyes were watching.

He was staring out at the pool, eager to get on with it, when he spotted her. Man alive, he thought, unable to tear his gaze from the woman, his normally cold heart leaping like a hot coal into his throat. Scores of beauties were slinking all over, but she was a world-class looker. Hell, no, he corrected, she was in a universe all by herself. Blond, not all that busty, but with long legs, the kind that were muscular in a gymnast way, tanned and displayed in the slit of her white semiformal evening dress as she strutted toward the gold lion.

Mr. Hollywood, he glimpsed, looking on, was less than halfhearted in his glory as he scribbled out an autograph for some kid who looked set to wet himself. The woman's face was classic sculpted angel, East European, maybe Ukranian, Harmon guessed from personal experience in that part of the world. The way she moved was all class, all woman, eyes front, boys, except for Mr. Right.

Sure enough, damn it, she wasn't alone. They weren't pawing each other, goo-goo eyes and such, not even holding hands, but Harmon sensed they were confident and sure in themselves, separate but together. Lovers, no question, and he hated the guy for just breathing the same air. The tall, athletic SOB on her wing was dark, maybe Italian, or just too much time in the sun. It was hard to tell with this bunch. Whoever he was, he didn't fit the playboy bill. The clothes for one thing, black slacks, matching dress shoes, aloha shirt worn out, dark shades, standard casual maybe, only…

Harmon's mental radar blipped louder the longer he studied the big guy. Something in the way he carried himself, an aura Harmon didn't trust. He sensed he was in the presence of another warrior.

Moving like the fearless lion king, Harmon noted the slow athletic carriage, only instinct warned him the dark man could move as fast as a cobra lunge, if the need arose. That wasn't any jet-setter. He tried to dismiss the troubled stirring in his gut as standard prelaunch jitters. But there was something about the man…

The drinks came, the big guy vanished and Harmon told the bartender to start him a tab.

"Did you bring it?" his companion asked.

They switched to French. Nobody paid attention to the French. Harmon downed his shot, sipped his beer. "I'll put it on the bar when I leave," he told the man, bobbing his head, grinning, just a couple of Frenchmen shooting small talk at the bar. "Quite the chosen. Truly an elite group."

"I have my reasons."

"I'm sure you do," Harmon replied.

"And the other matter?"

Harmon blew out a funnel of smoke. "In the package. We'll work out the finer details."

"See how things progress?"

"Took the words right out of my mouth."

"You understand that failure is not an option?"

"That's the only way I know how to work."

Harmon couldn't help himself, feeling stronger and more confident with each second. The man's cologne spiking his nose, the black op glanced at his comrade's face reflected in the mirror across the bar. Clean-shaved as smooth as a newborn's bottom, black hair closely cropped, the glasses a nice touch. Harmon turned his head, smiled at his swarthy companion and lifted his bottle. "Cheers. Here's to the party."

Jarrod Harmon touched glass with the man he knew had a twenty-million dollar bounty, dead or alive, on his scalp.

**2**

Father Jose Gadiz was disturbed. It seemed to take all his energy just to cross the vast expanse of gilded, marbled lobby and forge deeper into this so-called Heaven on Earth they had built for themselves. What waited was difficult. The anxious anticipation of seeing him after so many years, knowing the man's sins—which he made no attempt to hide, much less repent—broke his heart, sickened his soul.

The priest believed whatever he said would echo through eternity. That in mind, he clung to hope. Salvation or damnation, he knew beyond any shred of doubt, was the only guarantee. Not that he ever had reason to believe otherwise. But if others knew, he thought, then shuddered as the tentacles of the living visions reached out, reality suddenly obscured when the memory boiled up, shaping into what he so feared. And had so desperately been trying to forget.

He looked at all the handsome faces. They seemed to glow from pleasure indulged, rapture in the eyes, radiant auras. How their hearts, he thought, cloaked in the illusory shadow of satisfaction, the flesh kept sated by money, kept wanting more. Behind the smiles he saw lust, greed, envy, pride and a wrath that would trample anyone who denied them what they wanted.

All the lost souls.

It struck the priest their laughter was aimed at the world, perhaps what he stood for. A few of the more curious glanced at his white collar, the severe black clothing. Some appeared to shy away, as if embarrassed or afraid their hidden selves might be found out. Everywhere he saw bold desire, preoccupation with self, what they wanted. Had he expected any different? Why did he continue to live on in hope that he could somehow reach them, save, if only a few, from perdition?

Perhaps present circumstances had rendered him too harsh and judgmental right then, but he thought not. Perhaps the train ride had simply wearied him. Nerves shot, burdened as he was by Isadora's plight and suffering, heart crushed to agonizing pity as she urged this contact. Clearly, the way she had pleaded her case, it struck him she believed he was the last resort, the final hope.

He feared she was right.

And, just like that, it was as if he'd stepped into another dimension of time and space. Life slammed into a montage of freeze-frames. Somehow, he kept moving into the strange haze, aware he passed through white rays made ever more brilliant as they lanced through the stained-glass skylight. The living, such as they were, began lurching all about, faceless automatons. Their laughter swirled, hideous in ears that had heard the wailing of the damned, only the din now wasn't anywhere near as infinitely terrifying. Except for the rare few children, there was no light in any of them, even their flesh appearing like so much dark jelly. The more he searched their faces, the more he dreaded the world was in such deep trouble, so many so gripped in the power of evil, he wasn't sure if he was blessed or cursed, or strong enough to carry the message of what he'd seen.

Repent.

No human mind, he knew, could even begin to comprehend the depth and severity of the horror he had witnessed the past week. Not even he, a man of God—protected by divine guidance and assured salvation if he clung to his vows of chastity, poverty and obedience with unfailing perseverance— could fathom what he'd experienced.

The mere pale shadow of the memory nearly dropped him to his knees right then, shrieking blasphemies. He was mortified beyond terror just to think of them, as he tried but failed to focus on other words just to mute the faintest echo from his mind. There was an abominable stench of raw human waste, sulfur and flesh so putrified there was no smell—if he could even call it that—on Earth to compare it to, putrid fumes that still clung to his senses, stirring acid bile in his stomach. He'd felt the vicious clawing of utter despair that knew no depths or bounds.

Gadiz shuddered, became aware of his deep breathing, the strange looks as he marched on. Still, he felt disembodied, a man slogging through, then sinking into the sucking mud of a nightmare he couldn't escape from. As he wanted nothing more than to flee all of this seething impurity, before he was contaminated beyond hope, he hastened the pace, flying between walls of gold, grabbing a fleeting specter of his troubled, bearded visage in mirrored pillars. The ostentation of their exclusive realm became an obscenity to him, as he passed over marble then carpet. Giant crystal chandeliers speared light into his eyes, forcing him to bend his head. There were massive frescoed mosaics of saints, the Last Supper, conquistadors, too, in bloody glory over fallen victims. It was a sacrilegious display that galled him, all manner of luminous grand landscapes promising paradise on Earth for the monied elite.

Such a deadly illusion.

He passed the bustling wide-open area that marked the shopping mall. Ahead, beyond the bank of revolving doors, he spotted the gold lion, what he thought of as their Babylonian idol, overlord of the playland. So sad, so much waste among so much excess. The sum of it all, he decided, in such stark contrast to his poor village—those souls who suffered desperate poverty in brave silence and unwavering faith. He wanted to weep for the world, for the man and his estranged wife, for himself, and his own failures, for those personal weaknesses he had nearly succumbed to, but knew would demand a final accounting.

The faster he tried to reach his destination, the harder it became. Nearly racing for the doors, he spotted a fat man in a brilliant white suit and a blond woman in a leopard skin longcoat open to brazenly display a bikini underneath. She was young enough to be the fat man's granddaughter. They were veering toward him. Arm in arm, they were laughing for all the world to hear, what struck his ears as a loud and hideous screech. Two grim-faced men in black suit jackets were on either side, watching him from behind dark sunglasses. Their faces, all four of them, flashed into screaming burned demon masks, living images, no less, of what he'd seen in Hell, there, then gone. Gadiz gasped, fleeing their laughter as he bulled through the revolving door.

What was happening? he wondered, stumbling across the deck. Was he going mad? Had he been cursed by God? If so, why? Why did the blasphemies from the depths of Hell want to come shrieking through his mind, against his will? Was he to be tormented like this from now until the day he died and went to face his own judgment?

An angry shout sent Gadiz wheeling. He saw two dark

men, large black bags in their hands, their faces flaming with rage, teeth bared in predatory savageness. Apparently he had bumped into them without realizing it. He mumbled an apology. Staggering on, his mind crying out for God to save him, he heard vicious-sounding words hurled at his back, Arabic, he believed, cursing him he was sure.

What seemed an eternity later, he was past the large group at the gold lion, the world still, jolting around him in lighting flashes, demon faces, here and there, laughter…fading…almost human.

Trying to steady his breathing, he searched the tables, mentally counting off. Halfway down the bar, he spotted him, and Gadiz felt that invisible wall of ice envelop him once more. He felt a dark presence.

Forging into the surreal mist, two more demon masks flared in the corner of his eye, then he saw human faces slowly take shape, forming themselves as if invisible hands were molding rubbery features. Two men, sitting at the bar, a short dark man in glasses, his companion with white hair, cut short—military-style, he believed—a black bag at his feet. Both so grim, he sensed hatred and dark defiance at vast odds with all the carefree madness. Passing them, the chill melted away, then Gadiz felt a smothering presence of rage and hate, as strong as ever. The white-haired man was watching him; Gadiz felt the stare drill into the back of his head.

"How do you feel about including a padre on the roster?"

Did he actually hear that? Gadiz wondered. French? Familiar, yes, with the language, only it could have been Spanish, what with sight and sound blending into a living force, it seemed, distorting everything. And then…

He was heavier by fifty pounds or so than he remembered. The man was five years his junior, but the face he saw was old and tired, heavily creased but flaccid from the good life. There was laughter, faded as it was, in the dark eyes, but a cold emptiness betrayed to Gadiz a soul weary of the world but wanting to still indulge all of its pleasures. The gray suit was silk, the diamonds and gold on his fingers and around his neck the best his wealth, he was sure, could afford. Gadiz watched as he drank from a bottle of beer, swallowed a shot of whiskey, lining it up beside three empties, then gestured at the empty chair, snapping his fingers at the same time for a waitress. While the man lit a cigarette, Father Gadiz sat.

There was silence, then the man said, "How long has it been, Father? Five, six years?"

"At the very least."

"Father. Considering we never had one…that has a very strange ring to it, don't you think?" He paused, trying to comprehend something, then bobbed his head, a strange smile on his lips. "Father. Or can I still call you brother?"

**3**

Michael Charger saw them coming, all mouth and drunken swagger, but planned to sit tight, let events unfold as they would. Come what may, the tab could never be squared from where he sat. Still, all things considered—the coked-out temper tantrums, head-lopping of writers, directors and other key staff who were expected to make gold out of crap, what with the star himself barely able to throw a believable punch without umpteen takes, slow-motion choreography or computer graphics added postproduction—he figured to enjoy a live show where life might well imitate art.

The former United States Navy SEAL captain gave his two twenty-something buddies a grin, shook his head. The two knuckleheads came into focus from the east quad. It was crystal clear where they were headed and the object of their scorn. Roy Barnwell and Jimmy Rosco fidgeted, scowling. Charger could understand their dilemma. It was called job security.

Charger knew life in the fast lane of Hollywood was their only battlefield to date. At their tender age—with their fat paychecks—he suspected they feared the all-night parties with beautiful groupies and noses dug into conveyor belts of cocaine might skid to a screeching halt. Obscure in their profession, at best, he was sure they would be first in line to get kicked off the gravy train if something should happen to Bret Cameron.

The drunks in question cranked it up another decibel, pointing and laughing at Hollywood's latest hunk as they bridged the gap. Sid Morheim, Cameron's agent, became a human cannonball, shot out of his leather throne. The local groupies followed his mad dash for the photographers with squeals of delight. The tabloid flunkies smelled blood, no question, ready to cash in from the anticipated fracas.

Maybe the agent had arranged a publicity stunt to sell more tickets for the guy's latest sequel, Charger thought. As a soldier who knew the score in the real blood-and-guts world, this bunch came straight from planet Phony. In his experience there were no decent human beings in the movie business.

Were it not for who he'd been in real life, it might have bugged him to no end being the guy's stunt double. He was often mistaken in public for the star by beautiful young barracudas. There was some resemblance in physique, but the faces didn't quite match other than lean and mean hawkish. Age, for one thing, not so much in years, but wear and tear of grim experience under the fire of live rounds. Scars around the eyes and jaw from the kissing end of bullets were another problem, requiring touching up in the cutting room with computer graphics often switching mugs for any shot other than long. To keep Bret Cameron on top, superhuman tough for the world to behold, took three of them, and he figured they'd shared more concussions, burns, broken bones and torn ligaments, more stitches scalp to foot than many of the surviving war victims he'd seen in both Gulf wars, and beyond.

Charger could see his comrades growing more agitated to help Tyrell and Guamo run interference, but two things most likely kept them glued to their seats. One, they looked up to him, as the right stuff who had actually lived the kind of life the star only portrayed on the big screen. Two, they wouldn't mind seeing Cameron smeared by some truly righteous press if he got knocked on his can, and let Sid the Squid spin that. Rumors were the movie star had enough skeletons to keep his agent busy greasing tabloids as it stood. The little bejeweled, toupeed agent swept dirt under the rug often over any sordid mess created by their actor.

One of the drunks was out of the agent's stratospheric reach.

"Hey…movie star! Yeah, you, hero! How about an autograph?"

Charger lifted his beer, sipped, smiled. As the men moved for a close-up, their laughter took on a mocking note. One of them treated Cameron to an up-and-down look of pure contempt, then squeezed his package, asking his buddy in broken English why would such a big man need to pay underaged girls to lie to the tabloids about his sexual prowess.

Cameron looked stunned into paralysis by such disrespect.

The ex-SEAL suddenly wondered about that himself as he recalled whispered rumors how the star stayed so coked up Viagra was his only face-saving grace.

The show went on.

About five hundred pounds of steroid-buffed muscle, the salt-and-pepper bodyguards, made their move. The last of the teenagers, Charger saw, was scurrying off—or did Cameron give the boy a shove? The skinny kid looked flabbergasted, clutching an autographed poster like his ticket to paradise when he was nearly bowled down by Tyrell. One of the female hangers-on started giggling, looking hopeful for bloodshed. Sid Morheim bulled into the paparazzi, pink, diamond-studded fingers swishing away cameras. What Charger hoped would become a full-scale brawl, with Cameron on the deck, ended in only a short pushing and cursing contest. Reflex, though, spurred, no doubt by stung pride and a brain fried on coke, caused Cameron to wrench free of the blond trophies, step up and smash the challenger in the nose. It looked to Charger like one of Cameron's best shots, an award winner, in fact, that mashed beak, blood taking to the air from the burst faucet all but assuring a lawsuit. Worse still—Tyrell already had the drunk in a headlock, the cheap shot sure to have been caught on film.

Then a riot nearly erupted.

Guamo descended on the other heckler, speared a palm to sternum that sent him backpedaling in a lively jig step. His windmilling arms brought down a waitress with a squeal and crash of glass on the deck. The first drunk was squawking about assault, railing on about cops and lawsuits and sucker punches. Cameron was snarling some tough guy line from a safe distance while Morheim bleated at his meal ticket to stand down. Hotel security came flying into the tussle next from out of nowhere.

Charger looked away. He'd had enough. Money would change hands, the paparazzi film would be seized or they'd be briefed in private how it should play in the papers.

Charger put his full attention back on the blond woman in the white dress and her dark companion. For his money, both of them had stolen the spotlight in passing, moments ago.

Charger's nameless movie queen was sitting under a thatched umbrella, one long luscious leg crossed over the other, watching from a distance with a neutral look. It was her tall companion, though, who had Charger looking hard and wondering what his act was all about. The sun setting to throw dark shadows their direction, the woman's companion was all but obscured, nothing but a tall, broad specter. But Charger had seen enough, instinct shouting to the ex-SEAL this man was solar systems different, the way he was from Bret Cameron.

Another warrior, yes, sir, tried and true, in the living flesh.

YZET GOLIC WAS DISGUSTED. An ex-captain in the Serbian army, he was used to giving the orders, followed without hesitation or fail. Once upon a time the mere mention of his name struck terror into hearts, and anyone—Serb or Muslim—paid him due respect, unless they wished to see themselves and their entire families hacked to death or shot without warning. Entire fields and valleys all over Bosnia claimed the bones of Muslim men, women and children who had been shot simply for breathing the same air. Years after they shut down the prison camp he ran, NATO do-gooders were still tripping over skulls around Sarajevo, shouting his name all the way to the Hague like an obscenity. Spineless fools. The war he'd waged, he'd long since decided, was something only a Serb understood. And it had been like that in his country—ethnic cleansing of the undesirable elements—centuries before America had bombed Serbia into surrender. Who was he, only following tradition and orders himself, to question the morality of his actions, much less be judged by the West for trying to save his own kind? Hand himself over to so-called authorities for so-called atrocities, submit, forsake his will? Never.

Life had changed drastically since the NATO peacekeepers had marched in, maintaining what was an uneasy peace, at best, between the various ethnic groups. Someone had once told him change was good. Let that same individual tell him that now and he would pump a 9 mm round from his automatic pistol between the speaker's eyes. It was degrading enough an officer of his mighty reputation had been forced to become a common gangster in Belgrade, selling drugs, peddling whores, extorting business owners, just to survive. And with a sealed indictment out there, somewhere in Europe, with his and the old man's names stamped on it, plastic surgery had altered his once handsome face into a stranger he barely recognized in the mirror. As for the old man, nothing could change blubbery girth like a whale, the face of a baboon.

Changes, he thought, sounded like a sad song with an abysmal desperate end.

So, what was he now, he wondered, as he heard the witch demand he refill her glass with champagne. Beyond top lieutenant for the old man, it seemed he was expected to play the gofering eunuch for Mistress of the Month. Perhaps when they served chilled vodka in Hell, he thought. He had her number, thank God, and foresight enough to have filmed their brief but torrid liaison. It was leverage he was on the verge of using, if only to warn her she'd better show him respect.

Flicking cigar ash over the railing, he glared at the scuffle, wishing for his own outlet for all the pent-up aggression that had him seeing red. From the bird's-eye view twelve stories up he didn't need field glasses to read the situation. Security goons were dragging off two guests who were still flailing in their grasp, shouting obscenities. Suits from the movie entourage were gesturing all around the gold lion, shrugging at other tuxedoed hotel muscle, big shots restoring calm, ready to grease the right skids so they didn't get booted, or the incident sully their Star's name.

Well, he had hassles of his own, he thought bitterly.

A long stare out to sea, unable to count all the vessels, and Golic wished they were back on the old man's yacht. At least cruising the Mediterranean there seemed far less worry about constant vigilance against foreign commandos or bitter rivals. Any approaching craft was easy enough to spot, blow out of the water, if need be. As he searched the pool and its crowded deck, the vast garden and running bars, he knew any guest masquerading as some playboy could pose a threat. Perhaps the door would crash down with commandos slapping all of them in the face with those sealed indictments. Sure, they possessed bogus ID and passports. Yes, some of the local authorities were bribed into silence and submission, ready to alert them if a raid was being planned. But Golic felt the knot in his gut. Something was about to go terribly wrong.

"Yzet! Where is he?" the woman shrieked.

He clenched his jaw, willing the old man's return. There was business with some up-and-coming club owner in the city to conduct, a deal that would make the man rich beyond his wildest hopes, while cleaning their cash.

Already galled by what he knew he would find inside the suite, he strode through the open French doors. The old man was probably indulging himself with his whores, staying drunk, but meanwhile part of their duty was to guard the party albeit in envy from the sidelines.

He found her at the deep end of the massive living room, inside the open doors, stretched on her stomach on a padded leather table. Curtains fluttered near the glass in her outstretched hand as she enjoyed the view and the evening breeze. Ilina Kradja was beautiful, Golic had to admit, and as evil as the day was long. She repeated his name like some curse word.

"I need more champagne. In the kitchen. And open a new bottle. Go, damn you! Why do you just stand there like some idiot?"

Golic snorted, puffed his cigar, held his ground. He felt

the rage darken and boil, despised, too, the lust flaming in
his belly, trying hard not to stare at creamy flesh shamelessly
displayed. Whether for the envy of the whores—the scantily
clad trollops lounged on the huge horseshoe-shaped tiger-
skinned couch, or to amuse herself over the torment his own
soldier was forced to endure as he massaged her, it was clear
she was charged by showing off her stark nakedness. Having seen such an exhibition before, Golic could already hear
her wicked laughter when Nikimko, the masseur, excused
himself after the rubdown for a prolonged absence in the
bathroom.

When she reminded him of his lowly status, embellished
with lying taunts about his manhood and finally calling him
boychick, it felt as if the core of his brain erupted with hot
lava. He took a few steps her way then stopped and pinned
her with a cold stare. "Amazing," he said.

Through the thunder in his ears he somehow heard the
viper spit, "What? What is so amazing, boychick?"

A few of the whores, swiping at their noses, looked from
the porn movie on the giant-screen television to Kradja, then
watched him closely. Golic wondered why it had taken him
so long to work up the courage, as he told her, "You have everything a woman could want, but you are never satisfied."

"How dare…"

"Shut up! You are a despicable creature, Ilina Kradja," he
snarled, his lust firing to new and darker depths as she lay
there, trembling, shocked, speechless.

"You are a bottomless pit of demands. Unless there is endless money you can consume or much social stature to bask
in, men are nothing but peasants in your eyes, to be held in your
contempt, ignored, or trampled by your wretched existence."

Golic was moving away as she sputtered, "Come back

here! I will have your balls cut off and nailed to the wall for speaking to me like that! Do you hear me?"

He heard the door chimes instead. The old man's raucous laughter sounded as he came stumbling down the wide foyer, Krysha pawing him upright, brushing the white jacket. Vidan and Radic took up in the rear. Golic waited while the boss and his plaything of the hour moved down the steps. He could feel Ilina's smoldering fire, but knew she'd keep her mouth shut. Knowing her, she'd scheme of other ways to make his life miserable while keeping Dragovan Vikholic in the dark.

Impatient to discuss business, Golic scowled while the boss launched into a brief tirade about the hotel, cursing its guests and the slow service, but almost in the same breath laughing what a grand time he was having.

"Oh, my little princess," he said, slobbering all over Krysha's face, "how I wish I could stay here forever. Kiss Daddy with some sugar, if it so please you."

Golic tuned out the spectacle, wondering where the hell his life was headed, when he heard the chimes again. Vidan wheeled about-face and headed back down the foyer. Golic hoped it was the new pigeon.

He was moving away from the steps, about to clear his throat and call to Vikholic, when he heard what sounded like a loud thud. Instinct flared to angry life. Visions of commandos storming the suite taking shape in his mind like winged demons, he whirled toward the foyer, cigar snapped off between clenched teeth. He was digging out his pistol when he spied the object, spewing a funnel of smoke, before it arced overhead, sailing on. A glimpse of armed invaders in gas masks, then the acrid cloud swarmed Golic, legs folding as a black veil dropped over his eyes.

HAMID BHARJKHAN CAUTIONED himself against overconfidence. They were in. There was never any real doubt about initial penetration—Spanish operatives had been planted as employees a year earlier with the assistance of their financiers—but this simply started the clock. Head shrouded in a black hood as were the others. He unleathered the sound-suppressed Spanish 9 mm Star automatic pistol from his shoulder holster and marched off the private security-service elevator. The halls were clear, but why wouldn't they be?

He waved an arm and they raced into action. Two large bellhop dollies, heaped with black bags, rolled off the cage. Assault rifles were set on the carpeted floor, and two teammates went to work. One of them opened the panel, wiring the elevator car immobile, but slated to rise for the south edge of the lobby should the order come down, while the other freedom fighter, he glimpsed, was priming the plastic explosive for his radio remote box.

As he led the armed wave toward the open door of the main security-surveillance room midway down the narrow hall, he knew it was a moment to shine, absorb the divine power of Allah. How many months sweating it out in the North African sun, the endless hours of operational planning, running mock-ups? The forged documents, holing up, a day or so at a time, in cities across France, then Spain, to smoke out any tails. Bribing or forcing key individuals to get the critical wheels turning to pave the way, swearing them to secrecy under the threat of sudden death. Slipping their teams into the hotel as guests, with gear and weapons, two and three at a time.

The future was theirs to seize.

Point men for the dollies, four of his brothers hit the corridor on his right wing, AK-74s poised to blast anyone who wasn't where they were supposed to be right then. Stairwells, air vents that could double as insertion points from up top, the self-contained plant powering utilities, all were committed to memory from blueprints. The demo team vanished from sight, gone to rig the netherworld. In the event they needed to blow a crater, a series of massive explosions—or so the educated guess went—could take out the entire first floor. There was talk, during the final brief, that the blasts could so damage the foundation, the first floor and walls all but gone as support, the whole building could collapse. Recalling their laughter over what they envisioned as a possible miniversion of the World Trade Center, he only hoped he was clear when the floors began to pancake, shoving the image of being buried alive beneath tons of rubble from his mind as he led his six remaining fighters of Team Black to the door.

Two lagging behind to watch the hall, Bharjkhan charged through the doorway. He took a sweeping head count, believed they were all present, as his warriors barged past him, weapons raking the room. They were frozen, men and women in their seats or where they stood, eyes bulged in shock and horror. Someone screamed as his men shouted in Spanish for them to get their hands up and stretch out on the floor. Bharjkhan showed them a smile through the slit in his mask. They had been gathered there by the head of security to wait for a priority but phantom briefing on possible terrorism. As they stared back at their living nightmare, Bharjkhan nearly laughed out loud at the swift ease of the moment. Other than a suicidal fool, who would dare to stop them now?

**4**

"I think the movie star was the main attraction of that little scene. If I am not mistaken he hit that man when his bodyguard grabbed him. Bret something or other," the other beautiful woman stated.

The show over, Mack Bolan noted the entourage, ringed by added security, rolling in herd toward the hotel, presumably seeking shelter from any more storms. "I wouldn't know who he is," he replied.

"You are American. You never see movies?"

"I never seem to get the chance."

"Really. What does a retired homicide detective from Baltimore do with, I would imagine, so much time on his hands?"

"He starts over."

"In Barcelona?"

"Could be."

She seemed to think about something, then said, "Perhaps there is too much time, lonely time to pass. Someone you may care to spend such time with."

He nodded, sipped his beer. "I'm doing that now."

"Kat. You can call me Kat," she said, smiling.

He felt her stare, the stunning Ukrainian blonde probing him closely from the other side of the table. "I remember. Kat to your close friends, Katerina Muscovky to everyone else."

"Among other things to remember, I hope. And you, are you more than a close friend to Kat? Forgive me," she quickly added, turning away to watch the crowd, shifting in her chair. "I had no right to imply there is anything more than what there already is."

"There's nothing to forgive, Kat." He looked at her. "I couldn't have dreamed of time better spent with such a beautiful woman."

She paused, then, shifting gears, said, "You do not belong here."

A curve ball, but he kept his look and voice neutral. "How's that?"

She sipped her drink, weighing whatever was on her mind for a long moment. "I do not know…there is something about you. Different. You are not like any man I have ever met. Certainly not like these jet-setters and playboys, most of whom because of their money pretend to know what being a man is all about. You, on the other hand…well, beyond what is already obvious to me, I sense you are only passing through, coming from some place I could never begin to understand. Two nights we have been together, making love, and you tell me so little about yourself. I do not know who—perhaps what—you really are." She paused, and when he didn't respond, said, "I am prying, but I cannot help myself. I should know better, having seen both the good and the bad the world has to offer. You do not mind if I act like some infatuated teenaged girl?"

"Kat, there are men right now who would like nothing more than for me to drop dead just for the chance to sit here with you."

An enigmatic smile passed over her lips. "The way in which I caught the movie star look at me perhaps? Not that it would matter in the least to me. He is not a true man, only concerned about how he looks, whatever pleases him. I have seen fame, it does not impress me. What the famous show the world, what others think they love and aspire to be like is rarely what they get in person."

Mack Bolan thought she could have spoken no truer words. The ex-super model fell silent. She was done fishing for the moment about Matt Cooper, appearing content to watch the crowd, work on her drink, enjoy time spent together. The silence was comfortable enough, the kind, he supposed, shared between lovers where trust and respect didn't require an outpouring of talk to keep their bond from being severed.

He began scanning the crowd, nagged suddenly by a troubled feeling he couldn't pin down. Relax, reflect, recharge the warrior, let physical wounds heal, scars on the heart fade from witnessing firsthand man's inhumanity to man. Or so—urged by Hal Brognola, his longtime friend from the Justice Department—this brief stint of R and R was meant to do.

Strange how it never really worked that way, he decided, not in his world, where he would soon enough return. His companion couldn't possibly fathom the dark, bloody arena he came from. But she was right on one point. She was unaware of his real identity, the real man behind the concocted cover story he'd given her in one of the hotel's bars the night they met. No, he would never fit in with this crowd of rich and famous types, worlds apart even from the few vacationing families he'd seen. His own experience was light-years from this fleeting illusion where all was money, pleasure and bliss. Where life was just one big party.

Different worlds, no question, as day to night, life to death.

And they would never know it, of course, but the man also known as the Executioner waged a War Everlasting on their behalf, prepared, in fact, to give the ultimate sacrifice, if need be, so they could live free whatever their lives.

He was out of his element, he knew, a lion in a cage. Certainly it was not in his warrior's nature to kill time in a resort, rub elbows with the privileged elite while standing down. Similar in remote orbit, he supposed, but another universe removed nonetheless when compared to the humble man of the cloth he'd spotted. The priest struck him as if he wished he was anywhere but there, if he read the agitated body language right. And who were the loners? Six, maybe seven or eight at last count. Swarthy guys, hardly unusual for this part of the world, all with similar black bags in hand, smart business suits, strolling the pool deck, trying to look casual behind the shades.

Why couldn't he just unwind?

He recalled Spain was lately becoming an incubator for the kind of fanatics he hunted to extermination, a magnet for all walks of life, it seemed, legit and otherwise from all over Europe and Russia.

He'd been in France, and the chartered flight had allowed him to bring the Beretta 93-R and .44 Magnum Desert Eagle along, both stowed in a customized briefcase charged with an electrified field to jolt the curious or the thief into instant but nonlethal collapse. Bearing that in mind, he tried to will himself to relax but he felt a stalking invisible presence, one he knew all too well from sixth sense earned the hard and old-fashioned way.

"The hotel management is throwing a party in the ballroom for its guests in honor of its one-year opening. Or we could just order room service and..." He realized Muscovky was still speaking.

Her voice faded as Bolan spotted the white-haired man emerge from the bar. Just a strong hunch, but he sensed the guy didn't belong. The Executioner knew the type, having seen it countless times: a predator. Only this one, Bolan thought, was uneasy in his present appearance and environs but holding it all together around so much choice meat. The look was right, hard and lean, the gait military, but loose and oiled, proud of the way he could handle himself thanks to hard-earned experience. The man had a stare that devoured the model's flesh. A penetrating search lingered on Bolan, the guy doing his damnedest to figure him out, but coming up short. That same sixth sense told Bolan the man was dying to look back, but he kept heading for the doors, bag in hand, walking with purpose.

"Matt? Hello? Did you hear me?"

Bolan hoped the forced smile masked his inner rumbling. "Yeah." He cleared his throat, and said, "If it's all the same to you, I think I'd prefer just us. Unless…"

"No," she said, her puzzled expression softening into a smile. "It is what I had hoped you would say. So? Your room…or shall we use my place again?"

"Your place. The view's better," Bolan told her with a smile. He held the expression, feeling she wanted to push it, then she nodded.

He preferred to stick to her suite, lest she be tempted to ask questions, such as why, when he was so far from home, did he have only the briefcase and a small duffel with a change of clothes. The soldier considered stopping by his second-floor room, just the same. Then again, switching the weapons to his duffel, or putting the briefcase in her suite might only arouse female curiosity, questions nonetheless.

Still, all the dead enemies burned down in his wake, many of whom were sure to have vengeful surviving allies, friends or relatives—a chance encounter or stalking him—there was always the possibility, slim as it might be considering his surroundings…

Leave it, he told himself.

He felt that dark nagging again, thinking he should be within easy distance of his weapons, no matter what. Was it just old habits not wanting to die for one second? Take it easy, he told himself. Enjoy one more rare night off the battlefield with a beautiful woman. He reached over to take Katerina's hand.

"One more drink?" she asked.

"Sounds good to me," Bolan said.

**5**

The woman's sniveling about being a mother darkened his rage as her cries edged toward hysteria. Her ample stomach told him she was pregnant. Good, he decided. When they had something they were so terrified of losing—beyond their own lives, of course—then total compliance was all but assured. Her plight alone should make a perfect example to the others. Obey, or his wrath knew no limits, no outrage too great.

As the last of cell phones, pagers, IDs and walkie-talkies were piled in the far corner, Bharjkhan walked up to the woman and jammed the muzzle of his pistol to her forehead. She choked on her shriek, eyes widening in terror and the sound dissolved into a whimper. As she began to collapse, two of his men grabbed her shoulders. Yamil forced her up, barking curses and threats in her ear, shaking her out of her trance as Khajid finished fastening the dynamite vest around her torso. Suddenly there was a vicious curse, and a hostage rose from the group of corralled captives.

Yelling obscenities in Arabic, two of Bharjkhan's men pummeled the would-be hero's face and head with the butts of their assault rifles. Blood spurting as repeated blows pulped his nose, they drove the man to the floor, vicious kicks opening skin around the eyes and scalp until he didn't move.

"If anyone speaks or moves," Bharjkhan told them, grabbing the pregnant woman's hair and thrusting her face up, inches from his slitted eyes, "I will kill your colleague here and choose another to take her place." He let go, grunting for his men to take her out in the hall.

As he moved for the bank of security monitors, he ran a stare over the hostages. There were thirty-six captives, mostly men. All of them had their hands bound behind their backs with plastic cuffs, and had been dumped, facedown, on the floor. His black-clad men were planting blocks of C-4 primed for radio remote detonation around the room. In the event someone attempted to make contact before it all began, Bharjkhan would use the assistant head of security to lure them into joining the group.

The man who had made this part of the operation possible was being removed from the room. Fulfilling the charade, the bit player was squawking questions, pleading cooperation all the way out the door. The act, complete with bleating to at least release the women, had the desired effect on some of the captives. He heard a muffled sob, found two faces twisted his way, hate and defiance in the eyes. Filing away their faces, he decided they were next to be executed should there be any more interruptions.

"Do not resist and none of you will be hurt," Bharjkhan said, stepping in front of the security monitors. "All of you, just relax," he added, his tone as soothing and reassuring as he could fabricate.

Checking his watch, ticking down the numbers, he began looking at each monitor. The miniature cameras, he knew, were built into statues, hidden in palmettos and other shrubbery, mounted inside the frames of paintings or mirrors. Safeguarding themselves against invasion of privacy lawsuits, the hotel architects had not fitted any of the rooms or lavatories with minicams, but that wasn't necessarily a problem. Each floor, he observed, was covered from the south and north ends, double eyes for front and rear watching on each camera. Close-ups came with a twist of a dial on his panel, if necessary. The high-tech spying included the broad scope of the lobby, shopping mall, pool, all playground interiors, bars and restaurants. It was near one hundred percent visual precision, as far as he could tell, in both sweep and clarity. That the building's designers, he thought, didn't install cameras in the basement complex beyond the watcher's lair had allowed them to get in and take down the hostages, but could be a problem—perhaps a fatal one—if commandos responded.

However, breaching their defenses would be suicide. Unless, of course, they were willing to overlook initial devastating casualties. Again, he thought with confidence, no one, once warned, would be that daring, or foolish.

Bhajkhan plucked the handheld radio off his belt. "Abdul! Report." He scanned the lobby traffic, thinning out as people made their way for bars and restaurants. Spotting two men with black bags in business suits ambling to the desk, he smiled. Four other men he recognized from Team Red were lounging around the lobby, comfortable in big leather armchairs, smoking, reading newspapers or magazines. There would be others, he knew, some of them unseen until it started, but all of them ready for the big event.

"We are sealed in," came the answer in Arabic. "Should they pass through the motion sensors outside the service doors and stairwells—"

"Yes, yes. I want to know about the elevators," Bharjkhan said.

"As I feared. Even with our software program tied into the main engineering computer that powers their electricity, with the elevators constantly moving, we still need thirty minutes, perhaps more. We discussed this, the number of cars alone..."

There were eight banks of two cars, staggered at roughly equal intervals, east to west, north to south. Including service cars for staff, he was well aware of the numbers, understood the task. "You do not have thirty minutes," he growled. "Do it quickly and do not call me until it is done. And I do not want to hear any more about fear. Understood?" He punched off before Abdul could respond.

Bharjkhan felt the heat from anxiety rise, willing Abdul to hurry and complete the critical chore as he looked at his watch. The first sheen of sweat showed on his face. He glanced at the doorway when he heard the head of security cry, "No! Wait—"

He heard a muffled chug from the far end of the corridor, followed by the thud of deadweight. Bharjkhan returned to watching the screens. Just a few more minutes and he would become the great and avenging warrior of jihad he had dreamed about since fleeing the hateful occupation of his country.

**6**

"Why do you look at me like that? I am not sure if you despise me or…or what."

Father Gadiz, snapped out of the trance by his brother's voice, was unaware he'd been searching his face. Just what had he been looking for? The demon mask? There was no veil of diseased and burned flesh draped over Andres. Was there hope that he was not altogether lost? Was there some light still left in the eyes showing his soul had not been completely stained?

"Okay. You went through all this trouble to track me down. I take it you wish to relay a message? Tell me, did Isadora plead for me to come back? All is forgiven, we can live happily ever after?"

The priest felt his jaw clench. Unsure if he felt contempt, pity or anger toward Andres, he watched his brother gulp another shot, wash it back with beer, blow smoke. How pitifully tragic, he thought. All that pain and anger, eating up his soul, a festering cancer. Did he even care? The more he drank to calm the beast inside, the beast only grew stronger, soon enough to snap its chains. He could see that beast now, a warning beacon of rage building in the eyes.

"Speak, Father, please! Your silence is becoming insufferable."

"You do not even bother to try to hide this shame. It leads me to wonder…" Gadiz said.

Andres snorted. "If it was worth your trouble to come all the way here and try to save my soul from eternal damnation? If when the gates of Hell are slamming on my face I will remember how you warned me so?"

"You would be wise to watch your tongue, Andres. You were once a believer."

The priest fell silent, weighing his next words carefully, wondering if he should just get up and leave, stung to near outrage as he was by his brother's mocking. No, too easy, he thought, it was what his brother probably wanted. Further, there was his own accountability to consider, if he didn't harness the strength to persevere.

Andres, clearing his throat—was that shame flashing through his eyes?—inquired if he wanted something to drink. Oh, how he did, more than ever. He felt every flaming inch of his broken heart, the terrible burning ache with each awful pounding. He was tempted but declined.

Briefly Gadiz recalled the period where he'd indulged what had proved a near-fatal weakness in more ways than one. It had been so close, his own journey toward the abyss, teetering at the edge, so many nights wasted in an alcohol haze, questioning to near despair his own faith, his commitment to souls and to God. The young woman, restless and yearning to leave the village and her husband for the big city, had come almost weekly for confession. At her urging he began private counseling.

Where the Devil, he was certain, had conspired against him.

The woman had agonized over her habitual adultery, he remembered, but blamed her husband for the hateful trap her life had become. He had so despised his own thoughts toward her. He was wracked, worst of all, by such guilt and shame over his own lust, the bottle seemed his only relief from torment. Only the more he sought to drown the voice—the dark half of his own conscience, he believed—the more it urged him on, so persistent he thought he would go mad. He prayed almost nonstop for relief. He did not cave in nor pursue his desire, his only saving grace he was sure. But only when he stopped drinking for good, made his own confession, were his prayers answered. The taunting voice faded to nothing, the urge gradually died altogether.

"Your wife, she prays, but not for your return, Andres," he said, and saw his brother flinch, no doubt all that monstrous vanity shouting to him that such a thing was preposterous beyond all reason. "Isadora is a woman strong of faith. She is at Mass every day. She lights candles. She says the rosary. Where you live in lavish luxury, indulge all the pleasures of the good life you have acquired through your club or whatever else…she barely has bread and water to sustain her life."

Scowling, Andres broke eye contact. "What would you have me do? If it's money—"

"You foolish stupid man," Gadiz said, jolting his brother with the sudden anger in his voice. "She does not want your money."

Andres spread his arms, truly baffled. "Then, what?"

Father Gadiz sighed, shook his head, but pushed on, saying, "I know you can see her, even if you have not thought of her in years. Picture her, kneeling before the crucifix or the Virgin Mother, praying for her own soul, but also that your heart will change, that you will renounce your ways and put them behind before it is too late."

He thought he saw something change in his brother's eyes, as his body went utterly still. "To her, Andres, your soul is the only important thing. That is how much she loves you. Your return to your wife, of course, would depend on you. But do it, I should warn you, only if your heart is right in the eyes of God."

He watched as his brother's features seemed to shrivel, eyes dropping toward his next drink. Were those tears he fought to hold back?

Andres swallowed more whiskey. He quickly hardened back to anger.

Shocked by the depth of his sudden bitter disappointment, the priest stood to leave, then Andres, almost in a panic, said, "Wait. Please, don't go. I don't know how to live."

Gadiz stared at his brother. "What did you say?"

Andres cleared his throat, cracked his knuckles, eyes cast down. "Will you sit with me? Please, brother."

Watching Andres closely, the priest sensed the torment. He sat.

Andres fiddled with his bottle of beer. "Do you know how much I hated him? How much the mere memory of the man makes me hate him? If I could dig him up…oh, but I'm sure you will tell me you pray for his soul to rest in peace, that God's mercy knows no limits."

"I understand your feelings, Andres. I was there. You mention infinite mercy, but likewise God's justice knows no limits. It's out of our hands, try to come to peace with at least that much. Are you so dead inside that you can't even hear yourself? That what you so hate you have now become."

"Which is what? A drunkard, a philanderer, a hedonistic scoundrel?"

"Yes," Gadiz replied.

"I never beat Isadora within an inch of her life like he did our mother—or us for that matter. I never even cursed my wife! Yes, I know how that sounds, me trying to justify both my hatred for him and how I am living."

"That is exactly how it sounds."

In a harsh whisper, Andres said, "I tried…I wanted only a family. Two…we had two sons."

"And I have taken that into account, but that does not excuse you."

Andres stared off into the distance. There was fire in his eyes when looked back. "Why? Tell me, what did they ever do to be taken, and so young, to die so terribly…and from an illness that to this day no doctor can name? And does she, for all her virtue and noble poverty, ever for even one minute feel the kind of anger toward God that I feel?"

"If she did, I am unaware of it, and certainly her actions speak for how she feels in her heart," the priest replied.

"Which is what? That it was God's will our sons were taken from us and that she was left barren? That it's God's will I have become so wretched? Do you have an answer for me?"

Gadiz did, but he wasn't sure his brother would listen, much less accept it.

"Tell me, Jose. I need an answer."

"I cannot sit here and claim I know God's will for your life. I know only what it isn't. It takes courage to do what is right, Andres, that much I know. Evil is easy. It is a broad path of unrestrained laughter and song and pleasure. Evil is a coward and a liar. Evil is an illusion that will grant you what you think it is you so desire, but the price the soul has to pay is beyond the worst of any and all horrors on Earth." He paused, wondering how to proceed. "Is there anything you wish for me to tell Isadora?"

Andres swallowed another drink, scowled, turned sullen. "Tell her whatever you wish."

The priest stood. "Goodbye, Andres."

"Wait!"

"What is it now? You wish to know about our village?" Gadiz asked, growing exasperated.

"Perhaps."

"It is dying like all villages and hamlets across Spain. Only the elderly and the widows remain—"

"And the few faithful."

"Yes, the few faithful it would seem. Most of the young, they have run off to the cities to chase, I fear, whatever their own illusions."

"I meant to say, you have come so far, stay. What kind of brother would I be if I didn't at least put you up for the night and feed you?"

The priest shook his head, turned away. "This place makes me very uncomfortable. I'm sure you have other plans."

"Wait a minute!"

Frowning, the priest looked back, anxious to leave, but he was suddenly overwhelmed by the pleading in his brother's voice.

"I may never see you again," Andres said.

"That much could well be true."

"I have a room here, and, yes, before you say it, it is a suite on the top floor. A spectacular view of the sea, you can relax after your long journey. We can order dinner. Consider if this is to be our last time together…"

The priest let out a long breath, closed his eyes, then felt as if his very soul was suddenly branded by an image of his brother's wife. What he knew from his brief visit with her was more than enough to bear. So clear in all its painful truth, it was as if he could reach out and touch her. Isadora sitting by herself that night, as always, in the cramped quarters of the small modest home she once shared with his brother. Eating alone, as always, if she had any food at all, grateful if she did. Praying before she went to sleep. He wondered if she ever slept at all.

"I have some business to conduct," Andres said. "But I'll make it brief, if I don't excuse myself altogether. If you could wait for me upstairs?"

"I don't know..."

"What is one night?"

Father Gadiz made the decision based on hope. "Very well."

**7**

Trust wasn't a word found anywhere in his playbook. But part of the deal now, it demanded unconditional trust, total submission.

As in his surrender to fate.

From Jarrod Harmon's standpoint, this was the real dicey stretch where it could all go south. Just in case, he had a trump card or two in the event some treacherous traitor reared his hooded head.

Let in on cue by the call from his cell phone with its secure line of the highest state-of-the-art caliber, Harmon allowed himself to be manhandled a few steps down the foyer. The faceless, black-clad two-man escort presumably made a show for any watching eyes—if anyone could even see from their positions around the ornately carved post and flanking statues blocking out part of the room—as they shoved him against the wall. First, they liberated his duffel bag, then relieved him of the Browning, one of them growling for him to spread his arms and legs.

"Take it easy," he hissed. "You do know who I am, right?"

"We do."

At least the assault rifles weren't aimed his way as they patted him down. A good omen for success all the way down the line, he thought. Then he heard one of the terrorists shouting for someone to shut up, or a woman would be raped then shot before his eyes. A gruff, heavily accented voice began cursing in broken English, issuing threats there was no hope in hell of bringing to fruition. Had to be the Serb boss trying to save face. Then the familiar crack of flesh-on-flesh from a re-sounding slap to somebody's face brought on hard silence, except for muffled whimpering by a female captive or two.

"I'll keep the one in my jacket pocket," Harmon told the two men, keeping his voice low as he referred to the Walther PPK, watching the dark orbs inside the slits, burning back at him with hatred. "And leave the hands uncuffed, just like I know the man told you to do."

"You are very confident of your position," one of the masked men said.

Harmon didn't like the sound of that, but he showed them a smile. "It pays to know the right people."

"For your sake you had better hope so."

"Let's do this, so you can get busy spreading your sunshine," he replied.

SLIMDER VERSUS SLIMDER HE called it, but only to himself and in a rare lucid moment when there was blessed silence in his head. No mistake, it was a schizophrenic dance through those talking minefields—phantom or otherwise—and on the best days. On the worst days he knew it was sheer terror and relentless stalking madness.

By far, he was having one of his worst days.

He heard the ghosts of the not-so-distant past howl, trapped inside his skull. Outraged and vengeful, as usual, but they were really dug in now, the specters shrieking so loud, it seemed, he was shaken to where he felt he'd burst out of his skin. Why wouldn't they just go away? He wanted to scream out loud, but was somehow aware he wasn't alone in the suite. All he wanted...

Leave me alone! he thought.

Can't do it, good buddy, one of the voices said. We know what you wanted. Hey, no need for the big-shot vice prez of Tampa Bay Bank and Trust to explain. It's a done deal, remember? Those real-estate investments hatched when the whiskey was going down, nice and smooth. All that free money funneled and cleaned through the Cayman Islands, both eyes toward the grand future, knowing the good life you envied in others would soon become more than fantasy. So, what's with the whimpering? What were you going to do? Sit behind a desk the rest of your life and count other people's money?

He wanted the thoughts to stop.

No, the voice went on, shut up and listen to reason for once in your sorry life. Pretty slick, by the way—I'll give you credit for that golden tongue—all those promises to the elderly, the Sunshine State still the Eastern Seaboard's promised land of milk and honey, the biggest real-estate boom to date on the horizon. How, if they jumped on board a sure thing, they could kick back and just smile at the setting sun of their lives, in lavish comfort they only dreamed about during their working years. Hurricanes? Saints forbid. All covered by this new platinum insurance purchased through the investment, not even a category five could wipe you out if you sign the dotted line with us.

Oh, God, what had he done?

Stop whining! So you cleaned them out. So a lot of the old buzzards were scraping by on Social Security. They'll be rotting in the ground soon enough anyway, but you have your whole life ahead of you. Relax, you've been lifted out of the ashes. And forget that cold shrew of a wife while you're at it, they'll never find her. Nice job, another salute, catching her asleep like that. No noise, a little struggle, though, when she woke up and realized what was happening. Using your hands like that, a gun would have been less personal, but think of the mess to clean up. Women, huh. They just don't understand, even when you kill them. All you wanted was a taste, figured you were owed, and you were right. So you squandered money on hookers and drugs, but at least you got some, still do, but more now than ever with all that cash, and for a guy who looks like...

Stop the madness! he thought, fighting to clear his head.

Madness? the voice queried. Stop the sniveling! Be a man. You made the choice, deal with it. This is what you want, this is what you get...

"Did you say something over there?" a female voice suddenly intruded.

The girls. They were looking at him oddly.

Get a grip, he told himself. They were too beautiful for him to screw this up, to send them screaming out the door as if they thought he was some psycho, gibbering to himself. Somehow he found himself at the wet bar, building another double whiskey. He cursed the violent trembling in his hand, then one whispering Slimder assured him it was just the shakes from too much booze. One down the hatch would get him right. What the hell was this next urging? he wondered, as he gulped the drink. Twitching, he gazed into the darkening expanse of the Mediterranean, the voice sounding as if it called to him from the sea.

I can't stop you. Do what you must if that's what you really want.

Do what? Jump over the rail? Give all this up? It was twelve stories down. It would all be over before he knew it, mashed to gooey nothing like the parasite...

Breathe slow, concentrate. Drink some more whiskey, the voice commanded.

And it faded. Thank God for the warm elixir flooding through him, drowning the voice. Hell, he thought, embracing the slow return of silent reality, any number of things could have caused all this maddening anxiety and agitation. He drained the glass, then reached for the half-empty bottle. All the pills he consumed just to heave himself in and out of bed these days. All the coke snorted. All the Viagra swallowed when he needed help in the pinch. All the booze required just to keep him standing some days.

No wonder he was going crazy.

Then he heard the two recently divorced thirty-something women giggling from the couch. How sweet life was, he thought, back to beautiful blissful reality, watching as they loaded more rock into the glass stem. Taut, tan bodies, a lot of flesh showing, what with the halters and miniskirts. All these years, a pudgy little slob like him, and he could only dream. But now…

He'd met them in one of the hotel's many bars and just a few hours earlier. They were staying at the hotel indefinitely, looking for action now that they'd shed the hubbies and kids. Starting over like he was, from Topeka or Iowa or some such godawful place he'd never have to see. Buying them drinks, plying them, then flashing cash—he never left his suite without at least twenty grand walking-around money. A stroll through the shops, big spender that he was buying the girls a couple of mink coats ordered through one of his many bogus credit cards. His personal coke supply sealed the deal, now he just needed to push the envelope some.

"James, why don't you come over here and join us? It's your stuff, hon."

"Yeah, you look like you could use one."

James, not Jim, or the always loathsome Jimmy. Hon to boot. His stuff. His Presidential Suite, the Eden Suite they called it. Lush tropical vegetation, flower garden around a small pond in the living room, live exotic fish optional if he wanted to dump one of the tanks. He was the new Adam, all right, only blessed with two Eves. Paradise adorned with gleaming white marble and gold trim, he had to keep the lights turned low or the blinding brightness would all but obscure such a heavenly view.

"James, did you order room service?"

"Huh?" he said as reality intruded again.

"The door. Someone just in came. Unannounced, I may add."

The women were scrambling to hide the goodies, Slimder wondering why he hadn't heard the caw and screech of wild birds that passed as the doorbell for this suite whenever it was rung or opened—

They came from nowhere. He heard the girls scream, then saw two guys in black hoods holding assault rifles bounding off the foyer steps.

"I have money!" It was the only thing he could think of to save them all from what was clearly a robbery. He dug out the wad of cash, thrust it out as they shouted in what sounded like broken English for the women to sit down and shut their mouths.

"He does. Lots of money! It's in a suitcase in the bedroom!" one of the women screamed.

"Take it. Just don't hurt us!"

"We barely know this guy!"

He wanted to run over there and slap them both, treacherous sluts thinking only about saving their own skin. But, as one of the hoods stepped his way, he realized the moment demanded quick and clear thinking. Sure, there was two hundred large in the suite, plenty more stashed away in numbered accounts, but the cash on hand was hardly a grain of a sand on the beach.

"Here, take the money," Slimder told the man.

"I will," he said, and did. "And the suitcase your lady-friend mentioned. But it is not money we want."

"Then what?" he demanded, confounded as all hell.

Slimder was sure he would soil himself when he saw the slitted mouth bare a smile as the faceless invader told him, "The sacrifice of all you cherish the most."

**8**

Intuition told her the man she knew as Matt Cooper was keeping a secret. Surely everyone had something to hide, especially when she considered the world of her experience, and thought about her own skeletons. There was nothing in the closet, she believed, so shameful or unforgiveable he would simply excuse himself and vanish from her life. But her past was best kept locked away.

She supposed he fit the profile, the wary cop eyes sizing the world around him, good guy versus bad and such, saying next to nothing at all about what he saw and thought lest he reveal something about himself, expose a vulnerability. From what she had seen of policemen, she remembered them as cold and jaded, often brutal. More often than not they were sleazy, drug-addicted or alcoholics, indulging so many other transgressions she imagined it was a constant high-wire act of lies and deceit, extortion and bribery to maintain such treacherous footing. Then again, she had lived in Moscow during her rise to stardom where most policemen were the prisoners of gangsters. And none of them, she recalled, fit the bill of tall, dark and handsome like the man she was with. Nor did Matt Cooper exhibit the first sign he was anything other than a gentleman who most certainly knew how to treat a woman.

No crippling vices or weaknesses had she seen. Most men, in her experience, threw their cards on the table right away, hoping to fill her bed. Fighting to keep the smile off her face, she slipped the magnetic key card into the slot to open the suite's door—no man, policeman or otherwise, was near a lover like the man beside her.

She knew there was much more beneath the strong, quiet exterior than he showed her, arousing her curiosity way beyond the norm. Rather, it was what he didn't say that had her wondering about the hidden self, his own demons. Questions—few as she fought to keep them—were deftly evaded, or deflected with pat answers that sounded somewhat rehearsed, and from his prior experience in dealing with women who were interested in becoming more than just friends or lovers. Beyond the simplest semipersonal inquiries of getting to know him, there were the big ones she wasn't yet prepared to ask—at least until she felt comfortable enough to reveal more of her life. Such as how did an American policeman afford to stay at a hotel where even the cheapest lodging was several hundred dollars a night? And why didn't he seem to want her to stay in his room? Was he hiding something there, and if so, what? Was there another woman he wasn't telling her about? How did he see himself and doing what in the near future? Rather—when she sensed the moment was right and had worked up enough nerve—what did he think about the two of them…?

She let the last question trail off, as she heard the rush of the waterfalls. Matt was holding the door open for her. He was glancing down the hall, a strange look on his face. She sensed the tension, saw the tightening of his jawline, something dark and primal flashing through his blue eyes, as if, even when he appeared to relax, there was a giant coiled spring inside. Whatever his experience—what made the man—he maintained constant vigilance against his surroundings. Again, why?

"They called it the Fountain Suite when I checked in," she said, trying to lighten his dark mood. "It was this, or the Marquis de Sade Suite. If the noise bothers you…"

He shook his head, holding the door wide but searching the corridor ahead. Something was eating him, she thought, setting off the cop instincts for trouble.

She entered the foyer, and it hit her.

Dmitri. That's who he reminded her of, the way he seemed braced for trouble—for violence—around the next corner. Yes, there was danger about him, she decided, but sensed whatever had created him had seared his soul with a deep concern about the welfare of others. Whereas Dmitri—arrogant, vicious and possessive ex-boyfriend—couldn't have cared less if another human being lived or died. If there were any redeeming virtues in Dmitri she'd never seen them, but he was a gangster, after all, so what had she expected?

She believed whatever forged this man was gathering an invisible angry force as he stepped inside and shut the door. Suddenly she was afraid, not of Cooper, but of some unseen menace he seemed to know was in their presence. Whether from the sounds of lightly crashing water or his darkening mood, her limbs turned heavy as the corridor seemed to rush toward her in a slow-motion memory.

She saw the young girl from a poor village in the Ukraine, all of sixteen and suddenly swept up in the nightlife of Moscow. There was Dmitri, promising her the world, with his status in a top crime Family and his connections to modeling and fashion design. As it turned out, the meteor to the top of her profession—magazine covers, television commercials and bit parts in European films, Hollywood supposedly in the wings—came with a heavy price tag. Dmitri proved himself the Devil in human skin. Whatever her fortune—what he didn't steal—and fame, they almost claimed her life.

The runway lights dimmed. And there she was, like some caged wounded animal, hooked on the heroin Dmitri had forced her to take. He had been terrified of losing his hold on her as the world took more notice of Katerina Muscovky. Day by awful day, his insane jealousy took on demonic dimensions, until her addiction became the only relief from the living hell of his brutal enslavement. Her career derailed. The phone stopped ringing, the cameras no longer flashed as the rumors— many of them true—mounted, until her depression collapsed into despair. Until the day, either with a full syringe of nearly pure heroin or using the razor blade, she was going to—

Sudden menace sprang from thin air, it seemed. She glimpsed their weapons, felt the scream trapped in her throat, then she was falling—or was she shoved aside? Her first thought was Dmitri had found her, but how could that be? Dmitri was dead, gunned down by rivals, apparently at the very same hour she had been prepared to commit suicide— or so she'd been told.

She found herself on her side, halfway into the hall closet, splintered wood in her face, something sharp jabbing her ribs. She heard someone shouting, "Don't kill him!"

Cooper!

It happened so fast yet it seemed as if time froze, as she peered at the mayhem unfolding at the edge of the foyer. One of the invaders was on his knees, clutching his groin, vomit splashing across the marble floor as he made angry sobbing noises. Were there two, three or more attackers? she wondered, gripped by terror as she tried to count the figures in black hoods, heard what she believed was a snap of bone.

Then, in the haze, she spotted Cooper. Another attacker was locked in his arms, hanging limp baggage, head lolled to the side. Cooper appeared to be using him as a shield, the assault rifle jumping in his free hand for a split second, flaming at the ceiling. Then something appeared stuck in his shoulder, followed by what looked another dart drilled into his neck. She was about to scream his name, when a hand was wrenching her by the hair, dragging her from the closet.

**9**

"Yes, I do see the resemblance in your stunt double."

Mike Charger groaned into his beer, then Sid Morheim was in his face, the agent's back turned to the group on the other side of the elevator. Bret Cameron, surrounded by his chosen trio of party bimbos for the evening, was too busy basking in his new and supposedly important friend's schmooze fest to notice anything beyond the groupies who were giggling, awed by his every word or facial expression. Cameron bobbed his coiffed head in parrot rhythm to praise and pledges of assistance in getting the hotel's cooperation to let him shoot on location for the next *Rogue Mercenary* installment.

Morheim dropped his voice to a whisper as he said, "After your noticeable and disrespectful display of indifference earlier, you could at least try to act like a man who is grateful to be in such a position of honor."

"You mean kiss the right ass like you?" Charger said.

The smile was all plastic, staged for the moment. "Stunt men are a dime a dozen. And, yes, if I were you, I would be well-advised to start puckering up," the agent replied.

Charger decided he could wear a fake Hollywood smile, too. "Well, you're not me, Sid."

"Thank God."

It was all Charger could do to keep from smashing his beer bottle over Morheim's shiny dome. Instead, he grunted, then sipped his beer, watching the numbers flash as they climbed for the top floor. What the hell was he doing here? Five minutes earlier, he'd been by himself on a barstool, free at last, sure the star, staff and groupies had left to pass the night away in typical Hollywood debauchery. Hell, they had three whole Presidential Suites to themselves. Why couldn't they have just stayed put, let him breathe clean air for a change? Somehow, though, they had tracked him down, Cameron clearly having dusted himself off after the poolside encounter with a snout full of powder. The whiskey fumes were so strong Charger was nearly knocked off his stool. With Morheim in his corner blathering on about how important it was they all go meet with this major shareholder in the hotel, who, of course, was such a huge Cameron fan he could repeat, verbatim, his most famous tough guy one-liners…

These should have been far and away the easiest days of his life, Charger thought, but why did it all feel like such a cross to bear? If not for his young wife, who was expecting their first child… The money, of course, was a huge incentive.

Screw it. He was getting sick and tired. Every day was one more endurance test, staring at himself in the mirror wondering what he'd become. Maybe he'd just quit, but then what? No way would Sharon let him go back to the SEAL life, not these days when the action out there was primarily black ops for someone with his skills and track record. He knew old teammates were right then hunting down some of the worst scum of the Earth, and just so this kind of Hollywood crowd could gorge on the banquet feast of the good life.

"What do you think, Mike?"

Charger blinked at Cameron, then walked a gaze over the

short, swarthy man on the other side of the doors. Whoever the big cheese he worked for, the guy was packing, and more than just the handheld radio. The suit jacket was loose-fitting but the bulge noticeable to Charger's experienced eye.

"About what?" Charger asked.

Cameron frowned. "About the rappelling scene we talked about."

Charger felt Morheim glaring daggers into the side of his face. "Oh, yeah, your big bang finish. The one where you clear out a room full of about twenty bad guys with more firepower than was used in both Gulf wars, then as you go down the side of the building you empty about ten thousand rounds into another army of bad guys who are either firing back from the balconies or on the ground blazing away. I'll assume you have some kind of slo-mo ballet in mind for all the real gory kills and close shaves you take."

Cameron gave his stunt double a funny look. "You sound like you have some problems with it."

Nothing but, Charger thought, wondering how many takes, how many close hugs with death he and his stunt team would embrace while Cameron powdered his nose or got a hummer from some groupie in the trailer. "We'll talk," he said.

"But you think it's doable?"

"Everything's doable, Bret," Charger replied.

Clearing his throat, Morheim stepped into the act, clearly wanting to deflect the uneasy moment. "Who did you say you work for, Mr.…."

"Ladkani."

"Arab," Cameron said.

"Yes, a Saudi national to be precise."

"No offense, then," Cameron said, "that my next movie

may involve me killing—just on screen, mind you—a bunch of your people?"

"No offense taken whatsoever," the Saudi businessman replied.

"I mean, it's just a movie, right? Not like I buy into all the garbage every Arab is a fanatic and terrorist," Cameron said, flashing his Hollywood smile.

"We understand your position. Likewise the man I work for."

Cameron bobbed his head, flashed the man another matinee smile. "I like you already. Sounds like we might be able to do business."

"Yes, and since my employer is largely responsible for this hotel's existence, and since he knows many influential businessmen in Europe and beyond…well, as I said, Mr. Cameron, he is most anxious to meet you. It could well prove, shall I say, a boost in this part of the world for your career, not that it needs it, mind you."

"Hey, I understand," Cameron said.

"Indeed. Not only will he be most honored to meet such an important movie star such as yourself, but he is in a position of great importance, trust me."

Cameron beamed. "Say no more. A man can never have too many friends."

Call it instinct, but something about the moment and the guy felt all wrong to Charger. Morheim wanted to push more inquiries, but the Saudi was on his cell phone, relaying a message to the other end in Arabic. The Saudi was smiling, nodding, but Charger saw a wolf behind all that humble servant jazz. Ladkani? The name seemed to ring a warning bell, but how many Arabs had he encountered in Iraq with similar names? Still…

When the elevator stopped, Charger saw the Saudi's hand

vanish into his jacket as the doors were opening. The beer bottle slipping from his fingers, the ex-SEAL made his move as the women screamed. He was lunging across the car, rushing straight for the Saudi's pistol when he spied the black hoods in the mirror. The sledgehammer right to a jaw led Charger's attack, the AK-74 going with the faceless attacker as he fell into the Saudi. In the frenzy of the moment, as a rifle butt slammed off his skull, the ex-SEAL heard the pistol crack and Morheim's bellow of pain. Charger fell and took kicks to the ribs and head. He tried to stand, but another slashing blow off his skull drove him back down. Through the hazy curtain, tasting blood on his lips, he spotted Cameron hugging the women to him like a shield. Another kick to the head, and the stage lights faded as Charger spotted Morheim somewhere in the darkening mist. The agent was kneeling beside him, blood running off the hand he held to the side of his head, shrieking something about his ear being shot off.

A blast to the jaw knocked out the lights.

## 10

When he saw the blood pooled beneath the body stretched out inside the doors, the nightmare became all too terribly real, confirmed his worst suspicions. Donny Wilson thought he would be sick as he looked away from vacant eyes that seemed to stare straight at him. Somehow—for the sake of his wife and two children, he believed—he choked down the bile in his throat. If he broke now, so quick to beg for mercy before he even knew what this was really all about, then what hope did they have?

For God's sake, he thought, he was just a computer geek! How in the world did this happen?

Up to then it had seemed like someone's idea of a bad joke. His senior business partner was notorious for such foolishness, playing out dramas, but not on an obscene scale like this. When the boss had handed him the whole vacation package—instead of the yearly cash bonus—he wasn't sure what he'd find when he trooped the wife and kids into the New Barcelona Hotel. Swank accommodations, as advertised, a veritable king's palace no less of beautiful women and playboy types on the prowl, it had seemed like a vacation dream come true. For a few fleeting seconds he'd wished he wasn't a married man. For that matter, he'd found himself wanting to be more than just a guy who designed computer programs for various businesses. Fantasizing by the pool only a short while ago—buoyed by whiskey and the sight of so much young nubile flesh in string bikinis—he was a strapping action hero like that Cameron guy his son was all ga-ga over. Beyond landing in this heaven in Spain where he could only watch and partake of its simpler pleasures—fine dining, strolls with the family through the city's museums, shopping trips—nothing had ever happened to rock his suburban Chicago world, one way or another. No extramarital shenanigans, not even a masturbatory excursion through some Internet porn, hell, his only vice was a cigar and a few Scotch and waters once a week. Certainly violence—what he was sure was an attack by terrorists—was something that only happened to other people.

It was all so fanastic in its numbing horror, he felt like he was watching the event unfold on the evening news, but where he and his family were the main attractions. Sure, the world according to the nightly anchors was a vicious, ugly place, where murder and mayhem and kidnappings in places like Iraq, Colombia or Israel seemed a daily ritual—but always over there! Damn right, it always happened to somebody else, but—

One minute he was with his family in their suite, getting ready for dinner, then the next thing he knew he was answering the door, a gun thrust in his face, men in black hoods and assault rifles rushing into the room. His wife's scream had been abruptly ended by the vicious slap.

"Let my wife and children go, please," he'd begged.

"Shut up and keep moving or I will shoot all of you!" a gunman shouted.

No, he corrected, as he was shoved ahead, stumbling into his wife, not a nightmare at all.

They were walking into Hell.

"Just try and stay calm," he told his wife, and briefly wondered at the even keel in his voice. Maybe had more courage than he gave himself credit for, he thought, as he found Sandy trembling but clutching Alice and Tommy by her side. Courage, at least, for now, unless and until…

"What did I tell you? Keep silent!"

It was all he could manage to shuffle on, not look back at those eyes burning with such hatred and rage. The mere sight of the black hood pushed forth another wave of vomit he gagged down. Stop it, get control, he told himself, as he heard weapons fire and shouting from out in the hall. They would not just murder them, would they? They were just a family on vacation, no threat to anybody, no real stature whatsoever in the scheme of world events. Then a voice of dread in the darkest cavities of thought whispered that it was, in fact, because of their innocence and obscurity they might well be executed. And because they were Americans. He was familiar with Arabic, through some of his colleagues at work.

Arab terrorists.

A thousand and one regrets seared to mind, as he tasted hot bile squirting into his throat. He should have listened to his wife when she tried to talk him out of such an extravagant vacation. They weren't jet-setters, just simple family folk. If he wanted the beach so bad they could go to Florida. He could have traded the vacation package for hard cash they sorely needed instead, money for college and so forth, but he hadn't worked up sufficient courage to confront his tightfisted boss.

As if he could wave a wand and change it all now.

"Make this infidel family the last ones!"

Whoever barked the order—infidel family—it suddenly hit Wilson that the four of them had been specifically chosen from scores of other guests. A fresh wave of nausea rolling over him as he suspected why.

Then he saw the other captives, as tears of rage burned behind his eyes. They were sitting on their haunches, backs braced against the running window of the balcony where the curtains had been torn down. An unconscious man at the far end had his hands trussed behind his back as knives flashed, shredding more fabric. There was talk, some of it angry, some questions hurled in voices rife with terror before they were shouted at to be quiet, weapons pointing to a few faces of what struck him as the defiant ones.

His legs growing heavy, each step like walking in mud, he saw about a half-dozen armed black-clad figures grouped around a table choked with laptops, cell or sat phones, a radio console with headphones and digital readouts claiming most of the space. Flanked by two armed men, they were marched across the living room. It felt as if the whole world had suddenly collapsed its weight on his shoulders, his guts ripped out, a helpless fish flopping under the knife.

Wilson searched the faces of the captives, looking for—what? Hope? Courage? There were maybe twenty to thirty hostages, an even split of men and women it looked. They stared back with faces ranging from terror and panic to anger and defiance. A bald guy, bleeding all over the carpet, he saw, was blubbering to himself, his hand pressed over an ear. Wilson wondered if the torture had already begun, filing away the image of the guy bleeding like a stuck pig as a reminder to do as he—his family—was told. Unless it looked as though…

He saw the movie star next, surprised, not sure what he saw at first. Women on each side of him, they were clutching themselves, sobbing quietly, their lips working in soundless pleas. But if they were looking to him for salvation Wilson could read the star's expression for what it was. They could forget about him, reality now all but looking to shatter the big screen hero into a blubbering mass. There he was, the man his son so idolized looking terrified—as if he wished the floor would open up and swallow him.

There was a priest, he discovered, but he had a different look on his face than the others. It was calm, Wilson decided, though his expression was grim, concerned, to be sure, but he was holding it together, even if the brave face was forced. The priest, he thought, likely clinging to but reassured in his faith, no doubt believed God would somehow save them.

Wilson wasn't so sure God was anywhere to be found at the moment, wishing next he could dredge up just the smallest portion of courage he saw in the priest. He was Catholic himself, but—

He saw tripods being unfolded, two cameras snap-loaded with compact discs. It was as if he'd been punched in the gut, the wind driven from his lungs. He felt his knees buckle then, his heart a jackhammer in his chest as one camera was aimed at the hostages, the lens adjusted by a faceless captor, he assumed for a wide group shot. In the vise of terror he formed a strange sick image of a hood standing before the hostages, teeth bared—everyone say…"jihad."

Wilson felt the nausea rumble, boiling lava in his gut. Suddenly he pictured those evenings in front of the television, glued to the set, rapt, but listening with a vicarious sense of horror and revulsion. How Arab militants treated their kidnap victims. How they played on the terror of their captives, using it, in fact, to further their agendas, as blindfolded victims begged for their lives to be spared. How many of them were eventually beheaded, their gruesome murders filmed, no less, for the world…

The room began to spin in Wilson's eyes, then he was shoved closer to the hostages.

BHARJKHAN KNEW IT WAS pointless to crunch numbers. The hotel complex was enormous, and it was impossible to seize all of it by brute force. It would be enough, he knew, if they held down what they had taken. Which was why as many of them needed to be corralled in large groups at almost the same instant. Nothing less than ruthless audacity and iron spine was acceptable.

He found that, and then some, as the floodgates broke open and the warriors burst forth, hooded, armed and shouting.

Still, as his eyes darted from each monitor, trying to absorb as close to a near perfect takedown of the hotel as anticipated, he weighed numbers against both the good news and the bad. An even hundred warriors, the bulk of them divided between five main areas of operations, with six martyrs, strapped in with plastique wraparounds, roving corridors or stationed at strategic ambush points. The attack points were staggered, top to bottom, end to end as well as could have been planned, given the layout. The number of hostages seized en masse, with rabbits factored in at anywhere from five hundred to a thousand. Frightened herds were fleeing in stampedes.

He could see that in a portion of the lobby, up and down the length of the pool, hordes of guests were tearing off in all directions at the first rounds of autofire. Panic alone should wreak initial casualties, he hoped, broken bones and such, as he watched the human tornados blow through other guests. Some were bowled down and trampled in the crush, arms windmilling across the screen as bodies splashed down into the pool, other racing blurs slammed off the gold lion, hurtled along as they were by the crowds. Hooded figures came dancing across the monitors, autofire flaming to cut off exits, with other short bursts mowing down several guests in their tracks, warning other infidel packs to freeze where they sat or stood.

Or die.

It was impossible to mentally digest the frenzy of action exploding before his eyes. Even more impossible, he knew, would it be to guard every exit, window or door down each hall and stairwell, or post sentries at every corner, nook and cranny. Going in, though, all operators had understood and accepted the logistical nightmare. They were forced to leave avenues of potential penetration for ambitious commandos. But the good news was that the opposition—when it came—wouldn't know precisely what was booby trapped or where.

Until, of course, it was too late. After any initial failed rescue attempt by commandos, they would realize it was hopeless, be left sucking on impotent rage, all but defeated.

Smiling, Bharjkhan looked on, as warriors triggered assault rifles and submachine guns over the teeming masses gathered in the Grand Ballroom, the planted catering team digging hardware out from behind the buffet tables. Human lightning, they bolted to seal off exits, fiery cones sweeping the air with quiet bursts, bodies spiraling to the floor, dropping from their tables as they obeyed. A security guard from the south doors lunged for one of their men, the AK-74 hosing down that fool in his tracks.

Their hell, he thought, was his paradise, and their torment had only just begun in the cleansing flames of Islam. Wherever he looked it was nothing but pure, beautiful chaos.

In perfect concert, Team Red fired airbursts around the lobby, guests tumbling, flailing to the deck. Another holy warrior, he glimpsed, charged the desk, his assault rifle chopping down the tuxedoed staff behind the long barrier as another black-garbed soldier rushed into the back office, his Uzi submachine gun blazing. Elsewhere a few bodies littered hallways, but again the operational planners had stated initial executions were necessary, if only to serve as a dire omen for survivors to comply, or else.

A fighter informed him how many elevators were in their control. On those screens he saw the assigned teams were bolting into the cars, slinging hostages to the carpet, or shoving them into rooms, pummeling the few fighters to their knees with the butts of weapons, or knocking them off their feet with a burst to the chest. As he watched their slitted mouths on each soundless stage, he could only imagine the vile threats, the pleas and cries for mercy.

All the rich fatted calves led to the sacrificial altar of Islam.

And he felt rage suddenly overpower him. Wasn't this precisely what the occupiers had done all over Iraq? Kick down doors, shoot to ruins and even blow up homes and mosques in the holy cities, Mosul, Fallujah, Tikrit, too many other places where too many of his countrymen had been killed in droves. Or worse still, imprisoned, to be degraded by American men—and women!—the whole world watching their shame. He hated those prisoners nearly as much as their captors for allowing such humiliation to even happen without attempting to kill the enemy barehanded, or, at worst, taking their own lives somehow.

So many doors crashed down, so much Iraqi blood spilled, so much shame, and for what? he bitterly reflected. So American imperialist warmongers could plant their bootheel on more oil spigots? Stake out yet more sovereign Muslim land so they could gradually spread their poisonous culture, the evil of their insatiable greed and their hunger to dominate other surrounding Islamic nations?

Behind one of those many doors his wife and children had perished because the infidels believed he'd been there.

Now it was judgment day, he thought. No more, no less. And they were about to announce sentence on these decadent, money-grubbing oppressors of Islam. These rich, self-indulgent pleasure-seekers, he seethed, apathetic spectators to the world's suffering and misery and grinding poverty. They couldn't care less how untold numbers of Iraqis—Muslims everywhere—were being slaughtered by their legions. And they carried on, living fat and happy and sated, looking forward to more pleasure and comfort, a gilded future wrapped like a giant gift in money and the best toys their wealth could afford.

Suddenly Muhdatal said, "The Spanish authorities and commandos of the Special Intervention Unit are on their way."

Bharjkhan smiled into the monitor as he saw more infidels drop to the floor in the Grand Ballroom. So many lambs, he thought, and wondered who would be the first blood sacrifice.

## 11

Mack Bolan had a grim idea what he would find before he opened his eyes. Whatever the knockout shots had been, he felt the adrenaline burn, hot and furious enough through his blood to clear away any lingering sludge from the drug. Anger pumped in rhythm to the beating of his heart—did the rest to haul him back to the land of the living. Sobbing and soft voices reached his ears next, followed by gruff demands for silence, then he heard Katerina Muscovky quietly calling to him as he struggled to sit up. The real world of hooded gunmen and hostages came into slow final focus. His thought, as he took in the suite, aware the two of them had been moved, was to free himself and strike back. How to do that was a damn good question that presented no ready answers.

The others might have been clinging to some faint hope of rescue or simple release, but Bolan knew from hands-on experience what their captors were capable of doing. They could hide their faces, but he read the eyes of the fanatic beneath the hoods. He saw the rage, hate, the fires of commitment to their warped cause, and death. For damn sure, they wouldn't think twice about beheading any hostage. Looking at the cameras on tripods, he knew he'd better find a solution fast—before the executions began.

Bolan felt the model's stare. He was grateful she was alive, undamaged as far as he could tell. She was clearly unsure what to say, had terror in her eyes, and he sensed Muscovky was looking to him for some absolute hope and reassurance, a salvation he was in no position to deliver.

For the moment all looked lost.

Bolan sized up the room, counting visible enemy numbers, marking off the hardware and positions as he felt the pressure swelling in his fingers, hands bound tight behind his back. He saw six shooters, but the Executioner strongly suspected there were more in the suite or beyond, that, in fact, what he saw was just a portion of a larger fighting force, the hotel and its guests the big prize they'd seized. The assault rifles of choice were AK-47s and -74s. Two of them had RPG-7s slung across their shoulders, grenades fixed to webbing, then holstered side arms, large curved knives slipped through belt buckles. Hardly insurmountable odds.

A glimpse of torn satin fabric and whatever feeling he could manage from the bindings cutting into his wrists told him they'd tied his hands with curtains, maybe bed sheets. Better than steel, he supposed. Then he sensed the model's heat, a growing wave of fear as her body leaned into him, her limbs trembling, one hand on his arm…

Her hands were free. And his feet, for whatever reason, were left untied.

Two in the plus column, then.

Bolan shimmied up on his haunches, braced his back against the floor-to-ceiling glass. It was dark beyond the balcony, he observed. He wondered how long he'd been under.

It didn't matter, and it was wasted energy to beat himself up for not trusting his instincts, taking his weapons into her suite when the alarm bell had starting to ring poolside. He was still breathing.

Why remained to be seen.

As far as the Executioner was concerned, that was their biggest, and what he hoped their fatal mistake.

Muscovky's mouth opened, but Bolan shook his head. She nodded, gave his arm a squeeze. Whatever the myth about models being all beauty and no brains, instinct told him this one was a fighter, a gutsy lady who in her short life had seen a few dark days and survived. She was holding up, but for how long? Everyone, he knew, had a breaking point. Even him.

His mind was piecing together a plan of savage attack, even if it proved his final act on the planet.

Shoving aside grisly images that would only dance circles around what had to be his sole objective, Bolan found he was the last one sitting on the far left end. How many hostages it was hard to tell exactly, same deal pretty much whether their hands were tied. Counting legs or feet he figured twenty plus, his fellow captives stretching clear to the opposite wall. Down the line, where heads poked up higher than others who were either shorter, slumped over or had maybe fainted there were a few surprises. The movie star, for one, looking set to puke. So much for the Hollywood tough guy, but Bolan already knew public perception in such a case was not reality. There was the priest he'd seen around the pool, wearing a brave but understandably somber face. Bolan briefly wondered if anything short of divine intervention would set them all free and unharmed. Some prayer, he believed, certainly couldn't hurt.

There were some wounded already. He saw a balding guy he'd spotted among the Tinseltown jet set by the gold lion when the shoving match went down. Scrawny frame weighed down with jewelry around an open silk shirt, the blood poured from the man's head. Scratch him off the list of potential fighting allies.

There was a man close to mirror image of the Hollywood hero beside the bleeder, and Bolan caught his eye as he turned his way. The guy had that kind of uncanny radar, aware he was being watched and measured, a certain indefinable something the soldier recognized as old-school tough and stand up. Stunt double, Bolan figured, holding his steady eye, the purple welt on his jaw the result of some initial struggle. The man's cool defiance sent Bolan signals he was in the game, just looking for his one shot. No question, he was way more than Hollywood cheese, the Executioner knew, reading him as ex-military with a few combat stretches behind him.

Okay, then, he wasn't all alone, at least in the thinking department.  .

Despite best of willful intent, Bolan peered into the grim immediate future. Beyond the suicidal maniac or psychopath no one, he knew, wanted to die, and certainly not in the humiliating manner in which he suspected their captors were planning. When the time came—and he believed some opportunity would show itself—Bolan figured to count on at least one other warrior among the bunch. He just needed to start the hurricane, however he could, especially if it came down to his last minute on Earth.

Bolan felt the pall of fresh terror falling over the group as he saw a body dragged down the foyer steps by another hooded gunman. Between the manner in which the head lolled to one side and the black-clad hardman who slowly stepped up to the group and pinned him with a stare, Bolan knew the corpse with the broken neck belonged to his hands. The body was dumped in the middle of the room, and Bolan felt the full probing force of several pairs of eyes behind hoods aimed in his direction.

Moments later, a small table was dragged into the living room. Another gunman emptied a small duffel bag. The contents looked to Bolan like passports, other forms of ID. Another terrorist set a large suitcase beside the table. The warrior's sixth sense warned him the captives weren't random choices. Whether or not it was an inside job, terrorists planting their own as employees, handing over guest lists, with the rooms being raided for both specific hostages and their ID, well-known Americans had been singled out, perhaps law-enforcement agents, as in his case…

It remained to be seen.

The man the soldier reckoned was the leader of this terror force kept staring at him, Bolan feeling eyes down the line now watching him, as if seeing him for the first time. The terrorist seemed poised to speak, then a voice called to him in Arabic from the radio console. Wheeling, he marched to accept the handheld unit.

As he felt the tension thicken, smelled the fear, the Executioner suspected the terrorists were about to make contact with the Spanish authorities, announce whatever threats if their demands weren't carried out.

Show time.

"YOU ARE TO ADDRESS ME as Allah."

Colonel Sebastian Alvarado blinked at the handheld radio, thinking he'd be damned before he'd kowtow to a terrorist scumbag. He wondered, too, how the hell the fanatic had cut into a secured military frequency.

As soon as the SOS had been sent, either by guests in flight or the hotel's switchboard, all of Spain went into Threat-Con Black. Following the Madrid train attacks, TCB was the highest terror threat level, created by his own Special Intervention Unit, Spain's secret counterterror special forces. In short, Spain was in virtual lockdown, with martial law a phone call away. Train stations, airports, bus terminals, ports, all were shut down.

Striding to the end of his black command and control van, he wished he could get up close and personal with the bastard. He was hatefully aware his slung Z-84 subgun and holstered 9 mm Star pistol were as useless as promises from a politician. Alvarado weighed the dire predicament, assessing strengths and weaknesses, what he knew. What he didn't know was more than enough, however, when it came to holding back a lightning commando storm of the complex.

Already he'd been informed by the American Embassy—a CIA operative having placed the call if past experience served him right—a Delta Force contingent was en route by helicopter. Northeast Spain was Basque Country, he knew, and since the region was a growing haven for both homegrown and foreign terrorists, the American State Department had pleaded its case to his government, offering assistance, training, weapons.

Given what he faced, he supposed he could use all the help he could get, only too much assistance could bog down or muck-up any raid, what with egos thrown into the mix. But there were Americans being held as hostages.

There were way more innocent lives hanging in the balance than just United States citizens, he knew, bitterly wondering why Americans seemed to think their lives were more valuable than others. Regardless, he was not about to cave to political pandering, international greasing, media profiling. Up to a point—he would determine where the line in the sand was drawn—he'd play ball with the American Embassy. But kissing ass wasn't part of his job description.

As far as Alvarado was concerned, it was about saving innocent lives.

Those guests who had fled in mass exodus when the shooting started—some of whom were being tended to by medics on the scene in the vast parking lot—were being grilled by his subordinates and Barcelona law enforcement. The alpha and the omega of his immediate problem was that he couldn't know soon enough—if he discovered at all—how many terrorists were inside and where, how many hostages, how much of the hotel they controlled, the ordnance and firepower…

"Colonel Alvarado, I am getting the impression I do not fully have your attention."

Aware it was dangerous to leave the bastard hanging too long, Alvarado scanned the deployment of commandos. Platoon strength times two—with two squads of commandos on the way, plus God only knew how many Delta Force shooters—his men were spread on either side, equidistant down the lot. In full body armor with Kevlar helmets, they were shadows positioned behind military and civilian vehicles. Others were dug in among tree lines that hugged the deep north and south ends, all assault rifles and subguns poised—fanning windows, lobby doors, the parking garage entrance, rooftop—with Omega Team One hitting the beach, moving in on the pool.

He looked up. The twelve-story façade was hiding a potential slaughterhouse. He saw it strobing against the light show of myriad police, ambulance and fire vehicles.

To his one o'clock, less than two hundred feet away between the wide gap in palm trees, he looked at the west bank of lobby doors where his first real fear stared back at him. There, dozens of hostages had been forced to their knees, hands and faces pressed to glass. He counted at least four hooded terrorists wandering behind their wall of human armor, the same kind of barrier, he'd been informed by Omega Team Leader, had been erected down the east doors leading to the pool. From where he stood, it looked as if they had it covered, but he knew, upon relentless scouring and whatever intelligence they gathered in the coming minutes, he would find a breaching point they had either overlooked or couldn't plug because of numbers.

On the roof, just inside the retaining wall, he knew there was a team of six terrorists with three RPGs, sniper and assault rifles. And there were two Gatling guns, apparently bolted down into concrete with hydraulic drills, covering the east side—pool, beach and marinas—and the west side where his command post stretched away for the city proper. Roughly at the midway point, he saw the leading snout of the big stainless-steel man-eater pointing down, the terrorist invisible from his angle, giving the weapon a slow fan, back and forth over his troops. Any penetration from the roof looked to be an instant death wish. Considering all the gunships patrolling the skies over the beach, other choppers on six-to-twelve-block sweeps north, south and west, with sniper roosts on apartment rooftops, someone was bound to get struck by a tactical bolt of lightning, discover an angle of attack he had missed.

"Colonel?"

It occurred to him they were speaking in English, which, he suspected, was for the benefit of the captive audience. "Yeah. I'm assuming you have demands."

"Patience, Colonel. We have time to get to know each other, and some of our hostages may have an eternity, but that will all depend on you. If it gives you any comfort, we are not Basque Separatists, we have no involvement with your ETA.

In your country's favor, I would like to commend you for seeing the murderous and evil folly of the occupying forces in Iraq. Having said that, as supreme leader of World Islamic Jihad, I will give you one warning only. Should you attempt to breach the hotel—and we will know if so much as one shadow falls on the deepest corner—I will begin killing hostages in large groups. Their bodies will be taken to the roof and thrown into your lap. I am sending out but one example."

From witnesses he knew they'd already mowed down some of the guests. Alvarado was about to point that out, demand any wounded be released, when he heard a woman's sobbing. One of the terrorists was shouting for silence as a female hostage was suddenly shoved past the hostage barricade. Her hooded menace, an AK-47 aimed over her shoulder, trailed her through the lobby door. She was crying, her hands tied behind her back, the terrorist shaking her by the hair and snarling for her to shut up when Alvarado spotted the red lights, blinking up and down her torso. She was wrapped with enough plastic explosive to take out the lobby. He cursed. The bastard was swinging her from side to side, as if displaying his human suicide package like some trophy.

"Oh, God, do something! Don't let him kill—"

"Shut your mouth, American slut! Or I will shoot you now. All of you!" the terrorist shouted. "There are more just like her all over the hotel. How many and where you do not know! Attempt to enter and all will die!"

Alvarado felt his guts clench with hot rage, watching the terrorist backpedaling with his human shield. He heard the handheld radio crackle. The SOB calling himself Allah said, "As you can see, Colonel, we are in complete control."

He was thinking the underground parking garage presented a possible weak point, when the terrorist said, "Should you attempt to enter the parking garage we will also know that.

Should you try to discover which cars are packed with explosives we will know that, too. Even if you are lucky enough to disarm one vehicle…well, Colonel, I think you can see your dilemma clearly enough."

Alvarado balked, scanning the vehicles around him, wondering how many cars in the vicinity were likewise rigged to blow. "What do you want?" he asked.

"What I want is for you to contact the American Embassy."

"They're already sending someone."

"For your sake and the lives of the hostages they had better not be American commandos. Any attempt to storm the hotel, we have enough explosives to bring the building down," the terrorist said.

Alvarado felt sick. He believed them. The operation appeared near perfect from their standpoint, from planning to execution, but Alvarado knew no plan—especially when it came to military operations—was without some flaw. They were fanatics, no doubt. What they did was create mass murder, spread mayhem and terror. With their mind-set, and his own experience in dealing with their savage ilk, he was sure they would go the distance, even if that meant killing themselves in the process. That made them even more dangerous.

"Deliver this message, Colonel. American forces and their allies are to be removed from all Muslim countries. I repeat, all Muslim countries. And all of our brothers in holy war are to be released without delay from American prisons around the world."

Alvarado felt his jaw go slack. "You can't possibly—"

"Within, twenty-four hours, Colonel. Not one minute more."

"That's—"

"You are wasting time, Colonel Alvarado, stalling while you scheme some attack that will prove hopeless and disastrous for you and the hostages. Any helicopters approaching my hotel will be blown out of the sky and hostages will be executed. You have ten seconds, Colonel, to clear the lot and to also order the men moving in from my beach to fall back and all the way to the avenue out front."

"Hold on a second—"

"Eight seconds. Seven…"

"I want all the wounded brought outside," Alvarado said.

"Five seconds," the terrorist replied.

"At least allow us to treat the wounded. Give us something as a good faith gesture!"

"Allah!" the terrorist shouted.

"What!?" Alvarado asked, his gaze glued to the lobby, positive the curtain on the horror show was about to lift.

"You are to address me as Allah. And I do not hear the spirit of cooperation in your tone, Colonel."

"Hold on—"

"Two seconds…"

"Listen to me!"

Alvarado was about to scream the name when the first sonic peals of thunder split the night. Before pivoting in that direction, he knew he'd find a blanket of destruction being rained down from the roof.

He held his ground for a long moment as several vehicles erupted in waves of flying glass and sheared metal. His commandos were nosediving for cover, hugging trees as the roaring tempest washed over an armored van, pounding it to smoking scrap in about three eye blinks before the hellish cyclone came blasting his way. Luxury vehicles were sheared of canopies and hoods like flimsy tin in its raging path. He hit the deck just as the hurricane pounded the hull of his van, the angry and panicked shouts of his men inside flaying his ears.

**12**

His real name was Bernard Weebl and he didn't want to die.

As he cursed the tremors in his hands and feet, he wondered if the other hostages could see how terrified he was, certain most, if not all of them, recognized Bret Cameron. If these people didn't stand in line to see his movies, they at least knew of the rugged, fearless action hero. He was world famous.

A flash of anger bolstered his own sense of importance when he compared who and what he was to the other hostages, sure their own lives were puny and insignificant at best. Whatever they were they certainly didn't stand to lose what he had, nor did they have any chance of tasting the sweet fruit of the glorious future mapped out before him.

It didn't seem right, the ignominious injustice of it all. He was only thirty-three years old, he considered. Life had always rolled out before him, all the world a magic carpet, everyone with open arms, smiling assurances, glowing praise wherever he turned. From high school then college star quarterback, to soap operas followed by Hollywood movies, his life had followed the perfect script. He paid people to take care of life's problems. But there was no one on his payroll who could help him out of this jam.

He heard his mind suddenly raging that it was impossible.

Why would these lunatic Arabs try to rob him of his life, all he so cherished that went with being paraded as a Hollywood megastar. He couldn't lose it all now, not any of it, it just wouldn't be fair.

What were they all thinking of him anyway, he wondered, good guy and bad? How did the women see him? He had glimpsed a look in the eyes of one of his playthings for the night. Wasn't it contempt or disgust he'd spotted? Or was it just his imagination, her own terror he was reading? Who would prove expendable, he fretted, if these terrorists decided to make a human sacrifice to their so-called holy war?

Mentally scanning the checklist—in case it came down to the most reasonable pick for a sacrificial offering in lieu of him—there was a family guy, wife and two teenaged kids. Who would miss a few more suburban clones anyway if the unthinkable happened? Then a priest and what might pass for his brother, one, maybe both of them certain to draw Muslim ire, if only due to the religion angle. There was a big dark guy in Aloha shirt and some knockout number at the far end. The man had been dragged in, unconscious, left alive after a struggle probably, but why? Maybe he was the example they were planning to use, any display of muscled rebellion to meet certain execution? Hope, faint but growing now, Cameron was spotting some definite possibilities among the group for the chopping block. There was a dumpy oily looking sort a few heads down. He was gibbering to himself, half-crazed from fear, most likely, two stunning broads with him and clearly way out of his league, unless money made up for what he lacked in the flesh. He struck Cameron as an accountant, maybe a used-car salesman—no great loss to the world either way. At any rate, he'd caught two of the terrorists looking pointedly in the guy's direction, discussing something between themselves. That in mind, so far he had to believe he was out of the fire.

Then there was Sid, of course, whimpering beside him about the ear, stewing, quite literally, in his own juices. Well, agents were as easy to replace as stuntmen, and he couldn't say he cared for Charger's attitude lately, but the ex-SEAL was gutting it out, sitting there, calm, stoic, eyes slitted, watching.

Damn, but he hated Cameron right then, especially when he recalled the ex-SEAL going for broke in the elevator while he locked up. His only reaction had been to hug the women to his buffed chest. But maybe when this was over there'd be some way to flip Charger's brave showing, swing the elevator stunt around to his advantage, depending on what happened, of course.

Charger had damn well better be thinking about more than his own neck, he thought.

The fear was eating him up.

If only to distract himself, or drum up whatever courage he could find, Cameron tried to imagine what he would do on-screen, if they took notice, boxed him in a spotlight he couldn't avoid. He'd played roles similar to this present crisis, where he'd crept up on hostages being tortured and held by lunatic gunmen, kicking down doors and spraying the room, both fists filled with submachine guns the size of howitzers. The bad guys were riddled with dozens of rounds, chopped to bloody death in long slow-motion tumbles as he delivered the lines and the women swooned into his arms.

But this was real. No second takes, no stunt double to handle all the risks to life and limb. No makeup artists to create the illusion of bullet wounds, deep gashes running wild and free with blood, no screenplay crafted for him to deliver the perfect lines after an especially gruesome kill.

Nothing but cold fear.

Even in its horrifying reality it all seemed to be happening to someone else, or as if he was watching the drama unfold in the audience, tense and nervous, anticipating all the plot twists and turns, eager for some big action to start. They'd all heard their captor warning there would be executions if a raid was staged, or some colonel didn't meet the deadline of twenty-four hours. The terrorist leader, smug, in-control, looked ready to laugh out loud just before the thunder was unleashed. The big guns shook the floor.

The real weapons were no comparison to any sound effects Cameron knew of, leaving him shaken as reality thrust its unjust sleight of hand deeper into his belly, twisting and grinding.

"I need you to select one of your group to wear this."

Cameron felt his heart skip a beat, certain the terrorist was speaking to him. Instead, he found the man demanding to be called, Allah standing in front of the foreign toughs. Out of nowhere, the hooded gunmen were spreading down the line, weapons fanning the group. Cameron saw one of the terrorists holding out a vest, lumpy with blocks even he knew were plastic explosives. The fat man was snarling something in his native tongue when Allah drew his pistol and shot one of his toughs in the face. Blood and brain matter spattered the glass, women shrieked, and Cameron felt his stomach roll over. The pistol crack chimed spikes in his ears, it seemed, as the terrorists shouted for silence, hurling obscenities back at the fat man.

Allah said, "Fine. I will choose."

It seemed to happen in blurring fast forward. The woman was howling curses at the fat man—coward this, bastard that, do something, Drago—as the sheet fell away, revealing a naked body he would have found exquisite in another setting. Before Cameron knew it, her face was slapped, her flailing body slammed to the floor, then her hands were bound behind her back, the vest fastened on. She was still screaming obscenities as she was hauled past the group, then shoved out onto the balcony where Cameron saw her captor forcing her to stand at the railing. He heard a soft chuckle.

Cameron thought he was going to be sick when he found Allah walking straight up to him. The terrorist looked amused about something, his mouth slashed in a thin smile. There was a piece of paper in the man's hand. Cameron thought he heard the terrorist say something, but his ears were buzzing like chain saws. He was aware all eyes were not only watching, but measuring the man, he worried, against the myth.

"Yes. I am talking to you, Bret Cameron," the terrorist leader said.

Somehow he found his voice. "What?"

Allah thrust the paper at him. "You are to read this statement I prepared especially for you, Mr. Cameron, American movie idol. Take it. I will not ask a second time."

Cameron reached out and gingerly took the paper as if it were a poisonous snake. He could control the shakes in front of this audience, his mind swarmed by so much screaming madness he didn't know who or what to hate more right then. He watched through a haze where he imagined his whole world was about to evaporate like so much mist in the morning sun, as the terrorist stepped aside, informing him the camera had placed him square in the world spotlight. "Look straight ahead and read."

Something terrible and icy inside warned him to read it all to himself first, eyes darting from the video cam several feet away, then back to the statement. He moved his lips, but read the first few words to himself: I, Bret Cameron, movie star from the United States of America, hereby condemn the evil of my country's warmongering imperialist aggression against the Muslim world...

"Read it!" the terrorist ordered.

Cameron choked back the croaking sound in his throat. As he swept over the next block of words, his horror only magnified: I have come to agree with my new friends in jihad that America is the Great Satan, and I, Bret Cameron, hereby denounce every United States citizen for their own cowardice, which allows by its indifference for the mass murder of Muslims being committed by its criminal military to continue...

"Your last warning! Read it out loud and into the camera now!"

Cameron stared up at Allah for what felt like an eternity, his heartbeat thundering in his ears. "Do you know what you're asking me to do? I can't read this!"

"Can't or won't?"

Amazed at his sudden defiance, Cameron gritted his teeth at the terrorist. "I won't do it!"

"Then, Bret Cameron, you must decide this instant if your image is more important to you than the life of one in your own group."

"SOMEBODY, PLEASE! WILL you get him a doctor! Can't you see he's been shot?"

She was still bawling, near hysterics and cradling the head of a man in a tuxedo to her bosom when he saw the terrorist march toward the booth. She was pleading for a doctor right up to the second the AK-47 erupted, the woman screaming as the body jumped in her arms as if wired to fifty thousand volts. Blood spattered her face. The terrorist shouted for her to get on the floor or be shot. She stopped wailing when she was slammed across the jaw with the butt of the rifle, dropped to the floor, out cold.

Strangely enough, none of the other guests—two, maybe three hundred or more strewed around the restaurant and its bar—reacted to the sudden execution beyond a few sharp cries of alarm. What were they going to do anyway? he thought, cursing the predicament in which he found himself. Like him, they were trapped, spread out from one end to the next, facedown on the floor, covered by roaming hooded killers who had already shot three or more in the opening seconds of the takedown. Murder right out of the gate, either malice and hate for all things West, or to make a statement their captives were damned, no matter how important they thought they were, how much money they had. A group of about fifteen had been rounded up to kneel in the foyer, hands behind their heads. He figured they'd be the first to go should some commandos with more balls than brains come blasting in. If that happened…

Well, he'd already spotted the walking time bomb in a black hood. And where there was one—assuming most, if not all of the hotel was under siege—there were more fanatics ready to martyr themselves.

As much as he wanted to drop his face on the carpet and make himself invisible, he believed they were looking for someone in particular, judging the scrutiny they gave each guest, what looked like a passport in one of the maniac's hands. And he had a strong hunch about the person of interest.

The briefcase beside him would be damning evidence enough, then there was the laptop in his room. Provided they found it, could crack the access code that then ran into a series of firewalls, his personal cyber files were a treasure trove of operations in the works and on the board. But that was the reason he was filtered through the American Embassy in Spain to begin with. Yes, he'd been playing a most dangerous game and from the start, a hide-and-seek of treason, in fact, that might find him spending a lifetime in prison under the microscopes of various American intelligence agencies, assuming, of course, he survived this nightmare. There was a good chance the terrorists already knew about man, machine and mission, but wasn't that why he was here in the Falcon Restaurant anyway?

Well, not quite, not this way at any rate.

There was supposed to have been a contact arranged by another cutout through one of the geniuses who had hacked into the Pentagon files, a faceless entity he'd only ever talked to over the secured line of his sat phone, but who had told him where to be and when.

He was ready for the vipers to start biting…

Son of a bitch. Three of them were heading his way, taking a stroll with purpose down the bar, as they searched each face in passing. If he was the one they were looking for, how did he play this out? Say they did know his identity, say his own role came to light…

The terrorist stood over him. He looked up into cold black eyes. The terrorist seemed to think about something, examining the thin wallet in his hand, then said, "Mr. James Talliman of the American State Department. I am most pleased to meet you. You are to come with us, if you wish to live."

# 13

He was tempted to tell them who he was, then decided against it. The moment spoke for itself. Later—when the operation was wrapped, scores of infidels left dead in the wake of his vanishing act, perhaps the hotel collapsing if he made the call to bring it down—it would be easy enough to send the videos by his network of couriers to Al-Jazeera. Whoever was lucky enough to survive the night would never forget the ordeal, much less his name when they finally realized who precisely had allowed them to live. Yes, even in rare instances of mercy he could weaken the enemy by its own perception of him.

He just wanted to bask in the radiance of their terror before he pushed it further. There was nothing in his experience, he thought, like holding the power of life and death, deciding whether to play executioner or benevolent savior.

Standing before infidels as nothing short of Allah himself.

It was, indeed, quite an elite chosen, he considered, smiling as the movie star squirmed in the spotlight, all eyes aimed toward this Bret Cameron creature, waiting to see what he would do. Most likely it would be. The man—if he could call him that—was just a puffed-up pretender, but he had known as much when he selected him from the original list. There would be a fate worse than death for the movie star. Whether or not he was aware, the camera was recording his role as cornered ferret, the American movie hero glancing around, eyes wide and searching for someone, anyone to step forward and save him. He seemed to believe if he sat silent long enough a hostage would be chosen for execution, sparing him both his own blood and the trouble of deciding the matter. This was what the Americans paid money and homage to? This was who they held up as someone to admire, emulate? Sickening and baffling to say the least, he thought, but the minds of Americans were always hard at work conjuring illusions, spinning lies, weaving all manner of distortions, and to advance their own evil agenda around the world.

His hand draped over the rhino horn handle of the custom-made knife. How many infidels or Muslims in name only had he kidnapped, then tortured, or killed in Afghanistan, the Philippines, Iraq, he wondered. The two women with the movie star began pleading for him to read the statement the sideshow enough to buy Cameron a few more seconds.

He left them to their frightened squabbling. He found it both amazing and appalling how desperately they all wanted to live, even at the expense of one of their own. Usually they begged for their lives to be spared, offering money to be set free. The former always provided a heady feeling of supreme might, the latter normally accepted if time and circumstance permitted. In those the hostage was, in fact, freed, but minus his or her head. Both the executions and whatever money was taken on behalf of captives only served to carry on the jihad, perform the will of Allah.

Looking at several faces, he believed he could read their souls, especially the ones who cringed, hoping he'd forget about them. It was as if the concept of death was never a consideration, something that always happened to the other person.

There were, however, a few noticeable departures from the

norm this time. At least five, maybe six of the hostages showed bravery, or perhaps they were simply determined to brazen it out, clinging to hope—false as it was. He considered the priest, or the family man he'd selected from the guest list turned over to him by inside assistance. Then there were two other men who caught his keen eye. He sensed they were waiting for an opportunity to strike back. The Serb gangsters fell into the defiant class, but he'd already shot one of them as his patience fled in the face of anger and pride he could not tolerate, not if he wanted to keep iron-fisted control. At the far end, there was the big American with his companion, the former model. He had decided to abduct the man at the last minute, having spotted him by the pool, intrigued by what he sensed was a will of steel similar to his own. He knew that would be a challenge to break. The man was clearly in a class all by himself, a fighter like the movie star's stunt double. They would keep until he decided it was their turn to take center stage, but courage and defiance— even in the enemy—was to be admired. Bravery alone had bought several of them time, might spare their lives altogether, depending on what happened, which face he chose to wear.

"Mr. Cameron? I am waiting," he said.

"I can't…I can't…"

He slid the knife free from inside his belt. The women gasped as he took a step forward and growled, "Since you value your own life and movie career more than the lives of the others, Mr. Cameron, pick one now to die in your place. Or…"

He gave it a few more moments, the movie star gaping back, the women beside him on the verge of hysterics.

"Just read it, damn you!" one woman cried out.

"They're just words!" another said angrily.

"She's right, and they've already shot my ear off! For the love of God, Bret, they're going to murder one of us if you don't!" Sid Morheim said.

Cameron turned on his agent, snarling, "Why don't you read it, then? Use your name while you're at it!"

"Take him," the terrorist said, and pointed at the agent with his knife.

"No! Wait! He'll read it!" Morheim screamed.

"No, he won't," the terrorist said, and waited until the agent was dragged, kicking and screaming, to the second camera. There, he was forced to his knees. "Or will you, Mr. Cameron? Last chance."

"Bret, do something," he whimpered. "Please…do what they ask…"

"He can do nothing, and he never would." The terrorist stepped in front of the agent, caught one of the women cursing the movie star. "Why are you so afraid to die, Sid Morheim? Why is your own life so much more important than anyone else? It will be over before you are even aware."

"Look, please, just let me go. I don't want to die…"

"Who does? What about all the Muslims in the world being murdered every day by the American military or CIA?"

"I don't have anything to do with that!"

"So you say."

"I'm just an agent!"

"Yes, that is my whole point. You are an agent, you help make movies that glorify what you want to deny. What's more you become rich off the lies and propaganda of your country and your films."

The sight of the man, blubbering on, at once disgusted and infuriated the terrorist leader.

He held the knife in front of the agent's bulging eyes, then stepped to the side, told the hooded man behind him, "Hold his head up and back."

"No, don't! Bret! Do something!"

The gloved hand reached under the jaw, then wrenched the man's head up. He was inching the blade for the throat when someone said, "Stop!"

Slowly, spotting the figure rise in the corner of his eye, the terrorist leader turned.

"Take me in place of him. Take my life if it will spare the lives of the others," the priest said.

HE FOUND HIMSELF FACED with a sudden interesting dilemma. On one hand, he thought, as he warned off two of his men as they moved toward the priest and shouted for him to sit, if he went ahead and executed the man it would give special credence to the priest's own religion, perhaps rally the world even more against Islam. That the priest was willing to die for his faith, offering his own life in place of a complete stranger, and a pathetic coward to boot, showed tremendous courage. He had to begrudge the priest due respect and admiration, despite his own hatred and complete rejection of the religion the man stood behind.

"Brother, I beg of you, don't do this!"

As his warriors pummeled the man who jumped to his feet behind the priest—brothers, as it turned out, the terrorist leader pondered the situation. No, he really didn't want a martyr of the Catholic church on his hands, and there would be no disputing that's what the priest would be, what with the act of ultimate sacrifice caught on film, if he went that far. Then again, the outrage such an execution would inflame was too tempting to turn down. The act alone would display utter and ruthless contempt and rejection of any religion other than Islam.

"Throw this one back," he ordered his warrior, the agent blubbering something and looking ready to faint when the blade was removed from his throat. He gestured with the knife that the priest should step forward as the agent was kicked in the backside, sent sprawling at the feet of his savior for a moment before he realized where he was and crawled back to his spot beside the movie star.

"MOVE AND I WILL SHOOT the woman!"

Bolan knew the rage in his heart to act on impulse had tipped his hand, as the terrorist backed up and leveled the assault rifle on Katerina Muscovky's face. The soldier froze, hammered back into reality as fast as the desire sprung forth to attack, which would have proved suicidal, and homicidal to his companion. To the woman's credit she kept it together, as Bolan felt her shaking against his arm. Down the line, through the roar in his ears, the soldier heard a range of reactions. Sobs and gasps. Pleas and a quiet vicious curse. More threats should anyone move. Then someone retched, as the terrorist leader forced the priest to his knees, another hooded figure indicating with his rifle that the priest should look into the camera, pray if he had to, but in silence. One of the women cursed the movie star, as the priest shut his eyes. Bolan was sickened and burning with a depth of fury he couldn't recall in recent or distant memory. The worst part was there was absolutely nothing he could do to stop what was about to happen as the priest, taking the small crucifix from his chest and into his hands, prayed out loud, "I believe in God, the Father the Almighty—"

"I told you to pray in silence."

"—Creator of Heaven and Earth, of all that is seen and unseen—" Bolan spotted the sudden change in the terrorist's eyes as he was disobeyed "—and in Jesus Christ…"

The soldier saw it coming. As the priest prayed on, a new depth of savage hatred flared into the terrorist's eyes, the knife shaking in his hand, his lips parting as if to bellow something. Bolan felt Muscovsky drop her face into his shoulder as the terrorist thrust the priest's head up and the knife swept down.

IT WAS ALL UNRAVELING to hell, and fast. The big guy had apparently been ready to rush the guns, but Michael Charger reckoned the dark stranger saw the woman's blood on his hands if he acted on blind fury. Charger was with the guy in spirit, and then some; should one of these evil bastards make a mistake—meaning they came within decent striking distance.

How would he pull off the seemingly impossible?

With his hands tied behind his back, like the stranger, Charger still figured between the two of them they could take out two, maybe three with some pistoned feet to throats, jaws, balls, before they were cut down. That should divert all deadly focus while in the process they shouted for the others to run. With luck, the others wouldn't freeze. Instead, galvanized by what looked to be the only attempt to save themselves, they'd bolt en masse across the room. If they were all shot down in flight, they would at least have the satisfaction and the honor of knowing they went out fighting. In a stampede for the foyer, with all the confusion, terror and rage of the moment, a few of them might make it out the door.

It beat sitting there, waiting to be next for decapitation.

For no more than a couple of seconds, the ex-SEAL watched the execution. He wanted to brand to memory a face of bravery in the act of ultimate sacrifice he couldn't recall ever seeing.

And he wanted this act of pure evil to fuel his fire for the coming storm he intended to unleash, one way or another, with or without help.

The hostages were quietly crying, cursing, vomiting. He couldn't blame them one damn bit for any show of raw emotion. He came from a different world than most of them, he knew, where violent death in all its atrocities was nothing new, though this experience of being helpless to retaliate against such grotesque evil left him with a sick feeling, an impotent rage he didn't care to know again. He couldn't even work up the first shred of contempt or anger toward Cameron or Morheim, nor blame them for the priest's murder. They were what they were.

Charger looked away as the terrorist leader let the severed head fall from his hand.

**14**

"I understand all that, Colonel. To go in blasting with night-vision goggles and looking to strike the fear of God in their hearts while they stumble around in the dark was never an option."

"Well, since you already know they have their own series of generators inside and we can't shut down the power to kill the lights, I assume you have another plan in mind where we may take them by surprise and limit casualties in the process?"

"I do, indeed."

"Do you wish to elaborate?"

"I will, indeed."

Alvarado waited on the man to do just that. The Delta Force leader remained hunched over the bolted-down table, poring over the hotel's grid-mapped blueprints, aerial and satellite imagery while working on a cigarette, alternately grunting and rolling clouds of smoke over the bank of computers and surveillance monitors.

They were in the Delta Force commander's oversized war van, parked outside the stone wall, burrowed into tropical vegetation now that all forces had bailed from what was a field of debris littering the deep front end of the lot. Alvarado, forced to put out of mind two KIAs and four wounded among his own troops, looked at the tall, lean Commander Zeno, cer-

tain that was his handle for this operation, since there wasn't
any rank of commander in Delta Force that he was aware of.
The man wore standard-issue black, he noted, from a sheathed
Ka-Bar fighting knife sheathed just above high-topped combat boots to a Kevlar vest, the webbing hung with grenades,
slots jammed with spare magazines. A shoulder-holstered Beretta 92-F, an HK MP-5 submachine gun with all the trimmings of attached flashlight, laser sights and sound suppressor
hung down his back. A com link headset was snugged around
a bald dome scarred in spots from close shaves in the trenches.

Alvarado figured the Delta Force team to be at platoon
strength, one of Zeno's Black Hawks sat grounded on the avenue while the other gunship had joined the Spaniard's own
chopper in a sweep and recon of the Barcelona skies. Alvarado
had received his Presidential Directive moments before Delta
Force landed. It was a joint operation, but the Delta Force commander was to call tactics and to initiate first actionable contact with the terrorists. Political translation—if the situation
turned into a debacle and bodies were being wheeled out by
the dozens for a watching world or the hotel was blown into a
smoking heap, the Americans would take full responsibility.

There was another question facing them which could determine how and when they moved on the hotel. One of the
Delta Force techs, Alvarado saw, was still tapping on his keyboard like a master pianist, lines squiggling over his monitor.
What the bastard calling himself Allah didn't know, he
thought, was that his voice had been recorded on the minica-
sette built into his handheld unit. If the voice matched any terrorist currently in the top ten of the world's most wanted...

"Skubie?" Zeno suddenly asked the technician, as if his
reading his mind, the commander locked on to his intense pe-
rusing of blueprints beneath a funnel of smoke.

Alvarado felt his impatience growing, as one of the other commandos tapped Skubie on the shoulder, since he couldn't hear the Delta Force leader through the headphones.

"Commander?"

"Yes, Colonel. I haven't forgotten your question."

"Then I am sure you are of the opinion time is not on our side."

"I am, indeed. The longer we wait to make our move, the deeper they dig in, the more brazen they'll get. No matter how this plays out, Colonel, we can expect casualties. The only question is, how many on which side." The Delta Force commander straightened, glared at Skubie's back. The commando, as if feeling the eyes drilling into the back of his head, held up a hand, indicating he either needed more time or was on the verge of something. "Colonel, if it's who I think might be running the show on their end, then we can assume a worst-case scenario."

It occurred to Alvarado that they never mentioned the name of the terrorist in question, as if saying it was an evil obscenity. "Which is what?"

"You don't want to know. I have two Black Hawks on standby just north of the city proper. They will fly in on the hotel directly from the water, one from due east, one north. A diversion."

"A diversion?"

"A minor diversion at that."

"You intend to use your own people as potential targets while we breach—"

"Second," Zeno said, an edge to his voice as he blew smoke over Alvarado's head, "what you don't know is that we have a prototype unmanned aerial vehicle, an upgrade of our current Predator. It will disrupt all their communications. It will, in effect, neutralize all electronic and all radio signals that can set off ordinance."

"Which may well alert them they are under attack."

Zeno continued as if he hadn't heard Alvarado. "It's safe to assume they took down the security command and control center right out of the gate, or we would have heard from some hotel rent-a-cop by now. I'm guessing they had inside help, a very real possibility, considering the enormity of their task and the quick efficiency in which they carried out their assault on the hotel. Tactical logic, however, already told me the C and C would have been their first order of business. The U-AV I mentioned has been fitted with electromagnetic pulse superjammer that will shut down their cameras. They'll be blind, just like you wanted, but the window for us to penetrate and attack will be narrow. Six minutes tops before it flies on, out of range." Zeno blew smoke. "And, Colonel? I'm counting on them to panic."

"Come again?"

"Those potential targets, as you put it, may or may not come under fire, but they will draw the eyes of the team on the roof long enough for our snipers across the avenue to take them down. One head shot each, on cue, in rhythm. Their buzzard perch swept, one team drops, we breach from the ground."

"And that would be where?"

"I'll get to that, just as soon as we get all hands rounded up. I've got us a safehouse, about three blocks up the avenue, but we won't be there long enough to enjoy the view of the beach."

"If I may digress to your wish for the terrorists to panic. How will that help us?"

"Why, the screams and shouts of terror, Colonel. Of course."

Alvarado managed to keep the scowl off his face. He

found the American condescending, as if Spanish commandos were second-string talent. "I'm afraid I don't follow the logic."

Zeno blew out a long stream of smoke. "Colonel, how else are we going to pin down where large or small groups of hostages are being held once we breach?"

Alvarado scowled. "That's your plan? We follow the sound of weapons fire as they execute hostages?"

"If that has to be the case, and unless you have a better idea…"

"I hate to admit it, but under the circumstances I don't."

"I know your orders, Colonel, but I need to know right now if you're in or out. This could get real messy, 'career messy,' if you get my drift. And this is not one meant to be handed off to any politicians or some sniveling flunkies from the UN."

"Implying we will lose guests to the terrorists, no matter what the strategy."

"Or they blow the building and we lose everybody, including our people if all comes tumbling down."

"If you are asking does it bother me if a number of innocent people are murdered, sacrificed in order to save the lives of the majority—the answer is 'yes.'"

"If you want to watch our backs from the sidelines, that's up to you."

"No. I'm here to do my job."

Zeno was nodding when Skubie called out, "Sir, it's him, sir."

*Him,* again, Alvarado thought, only now that it was confirmed…

"Sir, would you like to compare the print—"

"I'll take you on your word, son, and keep that piece of information under your hat for the time being. That goes for the rest of you," he told the other commandos. "And you as well, Colonel."

Alvarado didn't like the sudden secrecy, aware now of Allah's true identity. "Would it do me any good to know why?"

"Not at present. Now, let's go nail down the details to the troops, Colonel."

HUMAN LIFE WAS A GIFT, and it was on loan. Be that as it may, Andres Gadiz had always viewed his own life as if he was owed, where he was an island, the rest of the world swimming around what he wanted.

As he spat the last of the vomit off his lips, aiming it into the puddle between his legs, it was as close to a bolt of lightning of revelation as Gadiz had ever experienced. It struck him—all too sadly too late—that he had never really known his brother, much less desired, given the crummy life he'd led, to fully understand what Jose believed in. Not only had his brother believed, but he had proved his faith before man and God, and so desperately attempted to persuade Andres to seek God in his final hours.

It occurred to Andres now that his brother had known something, seen "something" he was terribly afraid of, had been on the verge, he suspected, of telling him. The way he looked at the crowd in the bar earlier, eyes probing, burning, fighting back some fear of something only he saw—or imagined? Perhaps it could have been all the alcohol distorting Andres's perception, the moment exaggerated, puffed up on himself, as usual, to grand extremes, where he saw only what he wanted to see. Only...well, the dark searching look had become yet more intense when these animals had taken both of them hostage in the hall, and up until the second where...

Andres Gadiz choked down the slimy residue of acid bile.

And what of their encounter after all these years? he wondered, silently cursing the terrorists for not at least having the decency to remove the head and body from the hostages' sight, leaving both in the middle of the floor, so much garbage. The blood was still pulsing out, the sight an ultimate sacrilege he wished he could avenge, if not for his hands being bound.

If only Jose had left when he wanted, but he had to persuade him to stay the night, and what selfish impulse had compelled him to do that? Or was it some altruistic motive, something long since dead inside he'd been seeking to somehow resurrect? Had any hope he had to change—for redemption—left this world with his brother's soul? Out of nowhere, he felt the tears burning up behind his eyes, a fire unlike anything he'd ever felt, swelling in the core of his brain, spreading its searing wrath through every fiber of his being. He was shredded to wretched nothingness with agony and remorse, but the feeling was cleansing, demanding to release something he so desperately needed to find, to know, to cling to.

And what was that? he wondered. A way back to humanity? A return to God? Go back to his wife? Is this what it took, the very possible literal end, staring death in the face, where he was ground to collapsing implosion, into whimpering nothingness? Now that he was at death's door yawning wide, why would God even bother with such an abomination who had lived his life, safe to say, doing whatever he pleased, never denied himself anything?

If only his brother…if only not for his business with the Serbs, all of whom were in the same predicament… It was hardly any comfort now that the damned could enjoy one another's company.

If only, indeed.

If only his father had not walked out the door on all of them. If only he had not grown up dirt poor, forced to fight and scratch for everything he ever got. If only he had not abandoned Isadora, and if only his sons had lived. If only he had not chased money and pleasure and at the agonizing expense of innocent life beyond here that he himself might as well have taken by his own hand. If only he wasn't so damn weak and selfish he would not have forced this hand of fate, Jose would still be alive. Or had he simply brought judgment, the wrath of God down on his head by his own hand?

Life was not a game. When he thought about it, a man's few paltry years on Earth were little more than an eye blink in the unfathomable concept of eternity. Yet so many human beings—himself a prime offender and one of the worst of the worst—lived as if the laws of time and space and morality did not apply to them.

Jose, he decided, was right about evil. It was an illusion, it was easy, and that was its fatal allure. It was also selfish, and murder, he thought, the cold-blooded taking of innocent life, was as selfish as it got.

An image began to flame to mind as he heard strange chatter beside him. It sounded like a man's voice, somewhere beyond the two women on his left, but they were words he couldn't make out as he saw a pale shadow of his estranged wife on his last day in the village, Isadora, cloaked in radiant white and whisked off to Heaven while he was plunged into the burning sulfur of Hell.

"You must listen to me."

Gadiz was about to snarl at the terrorists to cover up his brother's body when he spied a man lurch to his feet in the corner of his eye.

"I have money, plenty more than what's in that suitcase, that I can give you!"

It took a full second for Gadiz to understand the man had

cracked from the stress of terror and panic, waddling away from the group, arms outstretched as if he was ready to hit his knees and beg for his life. The three terrorists closest to the man looked stunned for a moment, before one of them barked, "Sit down!"

"No, you don't understand! Listen to me, I'll pay you, you must let me go. You must…"

And he snapped, charging the terrorists, screaming at the top of his lungs as the assault rifles swung his way and cut loose.

BOLAN THREW HIMSELF into Katerina Muscovky, driving her to the floor as autofire chopped into the hostage. He figured it was bound to happen, some hysterical outburst, one of the hostages so consumed by mindless terror and fear of death he erupted into either desperate pleading or a suicide rush for the guns. Moments earlier, he'd heard the guy's whimpering reach a frantic pitch, his female friends demanding he be quiet. The soldier had been braced to act, and he beat the roar of autofire now by a microsecond.

They were shouting and screaming down the line, wild rounds blowing overhead, shattering glass. As he felt the hot slipstream of bullets tug at the back of his head—where Muscovky's chest had only a second ago been in the line of fire—Bolan spied the man grab one of the flaming AKs by the muzzle, two other streams of autofire converging to dice his expensive threads into chewed red tatters.

His full weight pinning Muscovky to the floor, the soldier was steeled for rounds to tear into his back, burst open his skull, end it all in one instant of madness beyond his control. As shards of glass pelted his head and face, Bolan caught the sharp grunts of pain as he saw the hostage kicked away by a boot to his gut, dancing and spinning under a full-metal jacket tempest. The man absorbed a few more flesh-eaters, then toppled, twitching out, the firing squad swinging weapons toward the group.

Bolan stared down into his companion's eyes. "You okay?"

Muscovky nodded, as fanatics bellowed for quiet. The order was not heeded, instead the panic grew.

"Sit up! All of you! Silence now! Or I will kill another of you without hesitation!"

Bolan slowly sat up, glass spilling from his hair. The terrorist on the balcony was screaming something in Arabic, AK pointing at the human time bomb stretched out at his feet, blood pumping from the woman's shattered skull.

"Leave her," the terrorist leader ordered his man on the balcony, then addressed his captives. "He was stupid," he snarled, lashing out at the body with a kick. He began to stride up and down the line, glaring at each face he passed. "Resistance is a death sentence. Now, because of that man's foolish act of suicide, one of you must decide who will replace the gangster's mistress on the balcony. Yes, that is correct. I need another human bomb in case a foolish rescue attempt is made on the hotel. And one of you I will select to become another star before my camera. No one is exempt this time. Whatever my mercy toward you before now has been exhausted." He paused, hooded stare walking down the line. "You have thirty minutes."

Another chorus of fear-stricken clamor broke out, but Bolan was concentrating on the piece of glass in the palm of his hand.

**15**

Colonel Alvarado waited until Commander Zeno gave the upraised fist, then led his troops away from the garbage container in a hunched, single-file toward the Delta Force commandos crouching at the base of the ten-foot-high wall.

Game time.

Despite initial grim reservations over what appeared a strategy destined for massive casualties, the SIU leader knew there was a tactical method to the Delta Force commander's seeming indifference to madness and mayhem. It was stating the obvious, he knew, that the terrorists had called the play, but the enemy's wanton show of savage force already had left them no choice but to counterattack with what was nothing short of a gutsy roll of the dice. Other than inserting robotic-moving cameras or gleaning hard facts from guests inside the hotel—both a reach to the moon when he factored in unknown opposition numbers, next to zero intel on positions and the ticking doomsday clock—the only feasible strike plan was being launched.

It would come down to timing, steely professional nerve, the best shooters, and, unfortunately, he knew, a lot of luck. Fortunately they had trained with the Americans—though Zeno was a new addition to the roster—but coming under fire as a unit would prove the only real and viable test. For that matter, all counterterrorist operations in his experience were won or lost in the first few seconds of contact with the enemy. In this instance, if their breach point was mined or enemy sentries were in the vicinity…

No time to fret now about what he didn't know or couldn't change. And when he considered the terrorist scourge leading the opposition, there was a good chance all bets were off once the shooting started. There was panic enough already, spread by the media and eyewitnesses, but if the name of the terrorist leader reached the wrong ears…

The insertion point for their Alpha One—two squads each of Delta Force and SIU commandos—was three blocks out from the southern facade where the hotel began to bend into a horseshoe. There was a small parking lot for employees just over the retaining wall, beyond which led to their private entrance. The door was always kept locked, but a tiny block of C-4 would gain them entry, Zeno wanting to bypass any high-tech chicanery with the keypad that might sound the alarm in the C and C lair.

Spotters and snipers on apartment rooftops, he knew, were monitoring windows and the hotel roof with night-vision equipment, heat-seeking handheld units able to paint an enemy position on their way up the narrow alley. All com links were tied in to one secured frequency which, he feared, may not be all that secure, but they'd made it this far. Alpha Two was committed to the north end, another narrow alley their marching path, which led to a walled-in area for service delivery trucks. Once both teams were in, their backs would be secured by trailing squads who would fan out—depending on what the fluid situation demanded—to take down east and west corridors the point teams had not secured. The working logic was that it was impossible for all entrances and exits to be manned by the enemy. They would need the bulk of their shooters just to maintain control over hostages. Between the guest list he had acquired and reports from witnesses, the hostage figure settled in at one thousand, give or take anywhere from two to three hundred.

A potential slaughterhouse.

Alvarado, with his sound-suppressed subgun leading the way, dropped to a crouch at the wall and checked his chronometer. One minute and counting until the super-UAV was within range to blank out cameras, hurl out a web of electromagnetic barriers to remote-controlled explosives. The commandos' window of opportunity was six to seven minutes to start taking back the hotel, free hostages, take out the enemy or it was the end of the game.

The two aluminum ladders were unfolded, the padded ends landing near the top of the wall.

Alvarado's headset crackled as Zeno's pilot informed them, "Eagle Scout to Alpha One, we have visual. Repeat, we have visual and they're taking an interest."

Zeno copied, then silently scurried up the ladder.

BOLAN FELT THE FIRST quarter inch or so of fabric give. Getting it started, he knew, was the hard part. Eventually determination would give him the raw strength necessary to pry his hands apart the deeper he cut.

And then?

They had bound right hand over left. There was just enough overlap to spare so he could dig the edge of the glass in, saw with the leverage of his fingers. Each puny dig and slice burned hope hotter, though, urging him on. It felt like a double wrap, the binding sheer silk, but that hardly made it any easier or quicker to slice. It was a grueling, agonizing chore, no question, as he was forced to keep one eye on six killers, fall into instant paralysis if they so much as glanced his way. Circulation in hands already numb was the least of his worries. In less than twenty minutes, according to his mental clock, another hostage would get beheaded. Fortunately the savage on the balcony had moved to the far opposite end, standing guard there, staring out to sea, as Bolan locked him in the corner of his eye. That, at least, left his back clear for the moment. Bolan knew Muscovky was tensing, but glimpsed her looking straight ahead. One squeeze of his arm to let him know she was in his corner, and she kept playing along in stony silence, sticking to the role of petrified hostage.

When his hands were free he'd seize whatever the smallest opportunity, and go for broke. If one of them so much as wandered within lunging distance…

Then there was the woman's body, the torso left wrapped in explosives, on the balcony to hurl into the touch-and-go equation. Most likely the cannibal outside had the detonator box, or maybe their leader standing just off to the side of the radio console. They had to be the first to go. Getting his hands on an assault rifle was priority number one.

There! Bolan felt another quarter inch or so loosen around his wrists, just enough flexibility by an agonizing but crucial degree where he could dig a little harder. He was thinking six shooters, no more, or they would have shown themselves from somewhere in the suite by now, when number seven gunner bounded off the foyer. He huddled with the head savage. They discussed something for a few moments in low whispers, two more extremists falling in to join them.

Bolan began a tiny slice into the bottom wrap when he saw the savage calling himself Allah go to the video cam. A freeze went down the line, a dead hush, but the terrorist extracted the compact disc, slipped it into his pants pocket, then quickly marched out of the suite. Whatever was happening, their leader gone for the moment, six killers remained to deal with. What the hostages did or didn't do when he made his play...

He had no choice but to go for it.

It stoked Bolan's fury and determination even more that they had not bothered to remove the priest's body. For all the soldier's intent and purpose that was good enough. The cold-blooded murder—and not even a clean decapitation at that, but instead sawing through the neck—was filed away in the Executioner's mind.

The priest's ultimate sacrifice, he determined, would not be in vain.

HE SHRUGGED OFF THE FIRST stab of panic as more instinct than perception of true reality. But Arim Palzahd felt something happening around him, a warning in the voices of his fellow warriors that the two Black Hawks weren't soaring in for a sweep of the beach.

They were being attacked!

Judging distance to the black shark-shaped gunships at roughly a half mile out to sea and closing from three or hundred feet up—one due east, the other veering around apartment buildings to the north—he knew they'd close to within striking distance in a matter of seconds. Manning the stainless-steel leviathan, he needed his orders and fast, and looked at Jabal.

Only Jabal was raging at the handheld unit, screaming obscenities for some reason. Palzahd found it an unseemly display of near hysterics for a holy warrior to so indulge, then it dawned on him Jabal wasn't able to patch through to their leader as he frantically punched buttons and static crackled across the rooftop.

As Palzahd turned to check on the others, a veil of cold fear dropped over him. He spotted Ahmad and Zarandij toppling from the other retaining wall, the Gatling gun hulking there, unmanned. The curse was on the tip of his tongue as he became aware of what was happening, the silhouettes of Takhamid and Fulahn spinning to the roof farther south, then he tasted the hot liquid spattered on his lips. Jabal was in free fall, face slamming off the wall, half of his head blown off. Palzahd slipped his finger inside the trigger guard. As he swung the monster gun around, lining up the Black Hawk streaking in from the velvet blackness of the sea, he felt the lightning hammer blow, a microsecond before it punched out the lights.

"YOU MAY THINK YOU know who I am, but if I were to tell you my true identity I daresay you would hit your knees and give me everything I want this second."

They had whisked James Talliman to a small bar lounge on the twelfth floor, northeast corner, he believed. It was a charnel house, bodies of men and women strewed all over the place, clear from foyer to the bay window overlooking the Mediterranean. Why one or several of them had gone berserk Talliman couldn't say, nor did he care if they volunteered their reasons. He was in a world of trouble himself, but he was still alive. He was queasy at the moment, all that fear doing a tap dance on his churning stomach as he tried but failed to not breathe in the coppery taint of so much spilled blood.

Staring at the new arrival, the State Department man found himself wondering about the voice, the eyes, the way the mouth was etched into a perpetual sneer. It was familiar, and he felt his stomach roll over again as recognition of the terrorist's identity was just beyond his grasp. No blindfold or cuffs, and they wanted to keep him breathing, no question about that. Good news or bad?

A dozen or so militants were staggered in twos and threes around the lounge, all brandishing assault rifles, a few RPGs hung from shoulders. Each man was weighted down with enough spare clips and grenades to hold off a small army of commandos.

Planning ahead.

But for what? An epic grandstand of mass murder and martyrdom? One of them, Talliman noted, had his laptop tucked under an arm, his briefcase clutched in the black-gloved fist of another hooded man. That signaled some hope to Talliman that he might live through the ordeal after all, regardless of the fate of all the other hostages. Looking out for number one could pay off, he decided, if he played his cards right.

Somehow, Talliman managed an even tone, as he said, "I gather you're eager to clue me in so that I can pledge my full cooperation for whatever you have in mind."

"In due time, Mr. Talliman, but I think you already know. And, no, the rumors of my demise were greatly exaggerated."

Talliman felt icy fingers of fear tap down his spine. "Disinformation."

"We do need to compete somehow with your side's propaganda. Understand me now, Mr. Talliman. Your life is only as valuable to me as your cooperation."

Before he could respond, there was a sudden commotion, voices shouting to one another in Arabic, a note of panic in their words. Talliman spotted one of the terrorists holding out a handheld unit from the foyer, static charges blistering the air.

"Control yourselves," the terrorist leader said, addressing all of them. "We knew this would happen, we anticipated a rapid response. It is but a minor nuisance. Do your duty, fulfill your obligation to Islam and Allah.

"Now," he said, turning to Talliman, "it is time for us to leave."

Talliman sounded a nervous chuckle. "I gather the building is being stormed and you expect we're just going to walk on out of here?"

"That is precisely what we are going to do."

BOLAN SENSED THE FEAR peaking to critical mass as the clock wound down. Blind terror might unleash another suicide charge, and before he was ready, as he saw two militants split from the group at the console, AKs sweeping the hostages, the extremists likewise picking up the bad vibes. They began slowly walking down the line, hurling insults, taunting the hostages to pick who would die next. Family man spoke up, Bolan amazed at how controlled his voice sounded as he nearly demanded they release his family, holding back just enough force where instinct warned him the guy was strongly considering giving himself up for execution—and probably would—if only they spared his wife and children. He showed guts, whether he followed through or not, but the soldier had a feeling he would go all the way to see his family live.

There seemed to be rising panic from the extremist front, as Bolan, heartbeat like thunder in his ears, saw the trio near the radio stiffen when static bursts tore through the suite to compete with pleas and sobs. They began arguing next, one of them pounding on the high-tech box as if a few good smacks would cure the problem. Unless Bolan missed his guess, the cavalry was on the way, having jammed radio frequencies before they swarmed into the building. If that was the case, then radio signals for detonators were also shot all to hell by the high-tech sorcery.

He had one chance, so close now...

Bolan put more pressure on the shard of glass the deeper he sliced, the edge nicking flesh as he twisted under the bottom wrap. He felt it yield a little, tearing a good half inch or more, straining his arms into pistons next, prying them away from each other, a test of sheer will against inanimate restraint.

The terrorist was less than a yard away to his one o'clock, he noted, wielding the assault rifle in what posed as one-handed arrogance, finger outside the trigger guard. Bolan ignored the possibility that he'd be discovered in the final seconds. This was it. Whatever came next he was going the distance. The Executioner concentrated every ounce of strength into his shoulders and arms, muscles tightening to steel cords.

Another eternal moment of pulling, wriggling...

There was the sound of glass breaking on the floor, a hostage crying out as the terrorist on the fear end shouted something, the militant closest to him spinning in that direction—

And his hands split free.

Bolan sprung to his feet.

It all became a blurring dance of death in the next second or two, adrenaline and the lava of pure hot anger exploding through the soldier's limbs, propelling them into action. Left hand flying across his body, he grabbed the AK-47's muzzle for a sweeping thrust down and to the far side of hostages. The hooded terrorist was in a half pivot, front and center, when the Executioner shot the heel of his palm into the tip of the man's nose, a lightning bolt that ripped forward at a lethal angle. Bone and cartilage splintered as the jagged mass speared into the victim's brain.

The soldier plucked the assault rifle from lifeless hands, the sack of limp flesh toppling in a sprawl to the side. The hostages were shouting and screaming now as two figures shot up from the floor in Bolan's periphery. Out of nowhere, the stunt double spiked a kick into the groin of the terrorist on the run from that direction, Bolan already swinging the AK-47 toward the trio at the radio console who were frozen a microsecond long enough to get drilled by his first sweep.

It was a flash of movement in the corner of his vision—as he raked the trio left to right and back, wild autofire on their end blasting the radio into smoking rubbish—but no sooner was the militant with injured testicles melting to his knees than the stunt double launched a kick square to the hidden face. The sickening crack of bone was audible through the din of terror and weapons fire, the terrorist lifted off his feet in an ungainly back flip.

As the last of Bolan's threesome began to pitch backward, short-circuited trigger fingers spraying AK airbursts, he surged ahead, tracking hooded target number six. The soldier was drawing target acquisition when he heard the repeated familiar crack of a pistol, discovered he needn't bother with the last savage standing. The terrorist bounced off the railing, jerked as another bullet tore through his hood, then he crumpled at the knees, a few last rounds of autofire blasting high and wide through the deep end of the window.

Assault rifle fanning foyer then bedroom doors, sensing a brief all-clear for the immediate present, Bolan turned toward the shooter and found himself facing White Hair from the pool.

BHARJKHAN CURSED. WHAT looked like a snowstorm was swirling across every monitor. With static buzzing from all handheld units and blasting from both radio panels he didn't need whichever warrior it was to tell him they had a serious problem.

Serious problem? he thought, and bit down another oath. Try catastrophe.

He knew what was happening but snatched the remote box off his belt anyway and thumbed on the activate switch.

The small glass eye stared back at him, lifeless, as he'd dreaded. He tried the second box that was tied into the room's ordnance. Same result.

The hostages sensed the change in the air, too, as he spotted hope flaring into several pairs of eyes, captives exchanging anxious looks, babbling in excited whispers.

"Silence!" Bharjkhan roared, two of his men falling over the hostages, echoing the order, waving assault rifles and subguns in their faces.

There was no point now, he knew, in raging about the oversight to bring detonation cord or time delays for the explosives, but he briefly wondered how the masterminds behind the operation could have neglected to see this critical detail for a possible Plan B. He had no problem being martyred, but with their network of explosives shut down, and presumably deadweight throughout the entire hotel…

Bharjkhan determined if this was it, commandos on the way to blow down the doors, then he would take whatever body count he could on his way to Paradise. For now, all his brothers in jihad, it would appear, were on their own against the coming adversaries.

But they knew how to play that deadly game, too.

They would execute as many infidel hostages as possible. Hit and run. Grab as much human armor wherever they could while challenging the enemy to the death. There was an escape hatch, yes, but it was way too early in the operation to even dare consider fleeing the complex. Or was it? Did he gut it out, confront whatever the crisis? Dig in or bail? And if the others held their ground, rode it out while he ran to save himself while whatever the trouble was taken care of, then he would be relieved of command with the instant permanence of a bullet to the brain.

Deciding to hedge his bets, he began shouting at his men to move half of the hostages into the corridor.

COLONEL ALVARADO'S TEAM WAS A dozen yards and closing from the maw at the end of the first-floor corridor running east to north—where he would spearhead his own troops into the lobby—when he briefly entertained Apocalyptic visions of the enemy's counterattack. It was unprofessional, he knew, to conjure up worst-case scenarios at this critical juncture when only the execution of rock-hard decisive action would win back the night. Still, he figured he wouldn't be human if at least the specters of murderous doom didn't creep into his thoughts.

He knew there was going to be panic, mass hysteria, where stampedes would erupt during the opening onslaught of weapons fire, the enemy mowing down people with indiscriminate maniacal glee, as was the wont of their savage ilk. The tactical play, however, demanded priority one the lightning takeout of any and all armed opposition before any focus on civilians. Medics were on standby, but they were ordered to hold back until each piece of enemy turf was seized back and secured. Of course, under the high-octane stress of what would prove rolling combat, he knew—despite all the diagrammed outflanking maneuvers and leapfrogging firepoints given the cover going in—each battle within the war was going to prove fluid.

In other words, once the shooting started, all bets were off.

The dam burst as soon as Zeno and two Delta Force shooters on his left wing cut loose with their subguns, the 9 mm tempest ripping into three black-garbed sentries posted at the pillared corners of their charge into the jaws of Hell. The design of the corridor—bending at a critical point where their advance was hidden until the last moment—proved fatal for the enemy. It was a fluke, Alvarado knew, but they'd embrace whatever good fortune came their way.

The militant trio—assault rifles stammering an impotent death knell toward the skylight but sounding the alarm—was in a one-eighty death spiral, a few more 9 mm rounds burping from sound-suppressed Delta Force HK subguns for good measure, when the lobby erupted into a maelstrom of utter pandemonium. Alvarado sprinted off to Zeno's right flank, dusting the first and closest hooded terrorist he spied with a quick burst to the chest, and the mayhem and murder quickly rivaled the colonel's expectations.

The lobby and atrium, complete with large, flowered shallow pits for group sitting was probably one-third a square city block, but laid out to computer blueprint as far as Alvarado could tell. Mirrored or marbled columns were staggered at twenty- to thirty-meter intervals. Roughly ten meters downrange, the SIU colonel tallied up six or seven militants, as a typhoon of autofire and screams blew his way. Half of the bastards, he saw, turned blazing assault rifles on a large group of twenty to thirty hostages huddled together in a bowl-shaped depression of couches, coffee tables and leather chairs. The other pack of their murderous brethren in the vicinity either grabbed human shields or bolted for cover, the slithering human serpents triggering weapons on the fly like madmen who knew the end had come but were hell-bent on going out in a blaze of glory.

A stampede began in full thundering earnest all over the

lobby, blocking clean lines of fire to several of the hooded militants who seized on the panic to vent their rage and frustration. Assault rifles and machine guns began hosing runners, the terrorist butchers sliding along, blasting away at the fleeing innocents. Bodies by the fours and fives, Alvarado glimpsed, were dropping all over, splashing into ponds and fountains, slamming off pillars, crashing to the floor.

Half of his commandos peeled off to his own flanks, firing while two three-man trailers forged past for the next point of cover. Alvarado surged ahead, subgun up and tracking, senses flayed by the clamor of relentless weapons fire, shattered glass, shouts and screams. He sighted on a terrorist midway down the lobby's desk, the militant's mouth vented in a soundless scream at the useless detonator box he shook in his hand. Three minutes now, give or take, and the colonel knew the enemy was back on-line, radio-remote explosives at their beck and call, the C and C able to track...

Stow it! Kill the enemy now, worry about the immediate future, if and when it arrived.

The SIU colonel bulled on as a mammoth palm frond was shredded by rounds a foot or so from the side of his face. Not missing a beat and braving the storm as flotsam rained in his path, Alvarado held back on the subgun's trigger and blew the gunner off his feet, slamming him into the deskfront.

One more murderous scourge down, he thought, subgun up and tracking the savages, but how many were left standing?

"THE NAME'S HARMON."

"What are you?"

"I think you can venture a decent guess. And you?"

"The name's Mike."

The big guy seemed to be deciding something. He glanced

at the pistol in Harmon's hand, but for some reason didn't seem inclined to question its sudden appearance at the most opportune moment or why he had it in the first place, as Harmon let the withering cries of the few innocent and the arrogant demands for release by the more insolent swirl by. That AK-47, still smoking in the big guy's fists, had moved an inch or so off his chest, but Mike Whoever kept measuring him with those penetrating ice blue eyes, peering, it felt, into his soul. Now that he was up close and clearly sensed they weren't about to get all that personal, Harmon wasn't sure he cared much for getting dissected like this by a man he knew now, beyond any doubt, had been down some mean dark alleys in his day.

Harmon could be reasonably sure—after his initial assurances to the hostages they would make it out of there unharmed if they remained calm and did as he said—the man was on the side of the angels. Which presented him with a sudden dilemma. Sure, the immediate crisis was over, Spanish and American commandos, no doubt, launching a major counteroffensive, as fit the scheme of things, and it looked shaky on his end for a few minutes there, what with the priest getting his head lopped off and the master of ceremonies…

"Grab an AK and an RPG. Watch the foyer."

The big guy was taking charge now, but what the hell, Harmon figured. The man, whoever, whatever he was, had earned the right to flex. The big guy walked up to the movie star's near look-alike, sliding a big fighting knife free from inside the belt buckle of his first kill along the way, Harmon was pretty sure he couldn't have blinked any quicker before this Mike guy flew off the floor and drove the terrorist's nose bone into his brain. He was faster than a cobra lunge, and the three terrorists at the radio never stood a chance either, dead on their feet before number one Scumbag dropped to the floor. Mike was a real dangerous man, Harmon realized, talented beyond measure in lethal martial skills.

Harmon saw that the radio had been shot to shit. He hauled up an AK-47, checked both of the duct-taped wraps of banana clips before plucking spares from another corpse, then slung an RPG-7 across his shoulder. He took a moment, watching the big guy working a little more to calm the hostages, walking to his ladyfriend last and offering her some words of encouragement. Mike said something Harmon couldn't hear next, but guessed he was telling her to stay put with the others, he'd be back for her, fear not, and such.

Great. This was not what he wanted, a real hero glued to his hip.

And as for his own role in the frenzied act of grabbing immediate salvation? he wondered. Well, it had been impulsive, no mistake about that, freeing the pistol and tagging the scumsucker on the balcony. He'd been forced to fall into yet another chameleon's camouflage, but playing the third savior just to keep the act going, well, Harmon didn't like the way in which the drama here had ended, certain where the big guy was headed next.

Out the door to headhunt, clear the way for the hostages. Swell.

Mike, he saw, walked on but glanced back, slicing the stunt double's hands free. Harmon caught the back and forth, the double informing the hero he was ex-SEAL when asked what he was before Hollywood. Again, it fit the action, Harmon thought, nothing but a King Kong pair backed up by hard-earned rep as he kicked the stuffing out of his victim with two lightning bolts from one foot, that militant DOA, by all reckoning, before he crashed to the floor.

Two bona fide tough guys.

"I want a gun."

Harmon glanced back at the suburbanite with wife and kids, saw that he was serious. The big guy briefly considered something, then told the ex-SEAL he'd leave that up to him, but the tone was clear enough that the family man had the right to bear arms.

Good enough, the big guy was bailing the suite, the stunt double left behind to hold down the fort. The movie star began squawking something Harmon couldn't make out, pressing deeper across the suite, but he did hear the real deal SEAL tell Cameron, "No, you don't need to say the words, Bret. I quit. You and Sid sit with the women and keep your mouths shut."

Harmon couldn't resist a smile, as one of the broads made a rather uncharitable comment about the seating arrangement amid Cameron and Sid. Man, but did he wish he could steal a few minutes to work the movie stud over as he recalled how the limp noodle would have let his agent die in his place. And just to save a career Harmon was sure wouldn't mean squat when the tabloids got wind of what happened here. Oh, but there were things worse than death, he thought, for some folks. Funny how life worked that way.

As he reached the foyer landing, crouched beside a pillar and picked up a faint rumble of shouting from down the corridor, Harmon considered his options. A solo flight was out, since he knew the score beyond the suite, gathered the only way out of the hotel was to team up with his new friend. A fighting withdrawal was questionable, when he considered the bigger picture, though doable, since dead men couldn't report to the hand feeding him he was responsible for sending them to the next world, which kept his own game in play, hope alive. Then there was option three.

He was thinking it best to maybe seize the iniative now, hose them all down—Mike and the SEAL first, of course— when he caught the big guy giving him a strange look.

"We've got activity out in the corridor," he called across the suite.

"I'm on the way."

Harmon saw the ex-SEAL hit the balcony, stripping the dead woman of the vest, then take the radio remote off the corpse outside. Meanwhile, the Serb boss, his surviving lieutenants and their chick parade, he saw, didn't cotton all that quick to Mike's orders for everybody to move out and hole up in one of the bedrooms. The gangsters wanted to be untied, but Mike ignored them. Harmon knew all about Drago Vikholic, and a Plan C was beginning to take shape in his head, if all else failed, depending on what happened on the way out.

The big guy had a few last words with the ex-SEAL—Harmon wishing he was a lip-reader—then he got busy loading up for war. An RPG-7 went across Mike's shoulder, then he took an AK-47 and checked the taped clips. He grabbed a handheld radio next, then quickly went to work claiming a combat vest and harness chocked with grenades and spare clips.

Harmon turned half of his attention to the end of the foyer, the noise of men in panic fading somewhat. This was a definite pain, he knew, all around, but he'd play it as it came his way, and he was the best at improvising under fire.

Hell, he was the Entity.

Harmon put the commotion at the window behind. He had his own world to save. The big guy was ready and coming at him, a small nylon satchel the dead would no longer need hung over his shoulder and bulging with what he suspected were spare clips and plenty of grenades. The big guy crouched across the way from his roost, scanning the foyer, listening to the muffled racket in the hall, weighing his next move.

"We going after them?" Harmon asked.

"That's the plan. I'm thinking a strike force has hit the building. We'll take out all the fanatics who cross our path. And there's only 'we' as long as you…"

"Hey, I've been down a few roads."

"Right."

"Trust me. I want to make it out of here in one piece as bad as you or anyone else."

"Trust, huh," the big guy said, nodding a couple times. "That's like money and respect."

"Yeah, I gotcha—it's earned. But that works two ways in this case, my friend," Harmon said, but the big guy was already up and rolling down the foyer, AK leading his quick march for the doors.

**16**

In the highly unlikely and improbable event they blasted a hole through the ceiling and jumped down, Bharjkhan knew there were only three ways into the underground complex, all of which were covered. Judging the thundering herds and muted waves of shouts and weapons fire above, he doubted the commandos had either time or inclination to break through from above. And, now, without the explosives at their command...

Were they doomed? Was the glorious dream of personal jihad, bringing the hotel down, about to die before its fruition?

And did he have manpower enough to tackle his own corridor? Bharjkhan wondered, two of his warriors racing to the far security and utility complex doors, assault rifles up and ready to shoot when the barriers came down, as he was positive they would. Even before he ran through the count of shooters he already knew he was short. Two warriors in the elevator, then six watching the north side hall. The security room under guard by another six, ready to execute all hostages...

He then heard the muffled peals of explosions and stammering bursts of autofire from beyond the locked door to the utility vault.

They were coming.

Silently, as he snugged the female shield closer to his chest, he cursed the detonation box, then offered a short feverish prayer, his burning thoughts imploring the will of God to show him the light. Then he suddenly remembered he had brought the remote unit to light up the C and C hole, instead of leaving it where it would do the most good, thus compounding potential disaster. He cursed himself viciously for what may prove to be a damning oversight, wondered if fear of failure was so working on his nerves he couldn't think straight. As if it mattered anyway, given the enemy had jammed their radio signals.

His assault rifle aimed one-handed down the hall, Bharjkhan was looking over the heads of the five hostages on their knees before him, hissing in the woman's ear to be quiet, when what looked to be the door to the utility lair was blown off its hinges, a mangled airborne missile that bowled down one of his men at the knees.

The enemy showed its hand a microsecond later, as the security door toppled into the corridor and muzzle-flashes began strobing through the boiling smoke. Dark figures appeared scrunched to either side of the jamb, subguns cutting down his two-man vanguard, blowing one off his feet, pinning the other to the floor in a splash of blood and tattered cloth. One of his warriors had the quick inspiration to trigger his RPG-7, but Bharjkhan glimpsed it sailing off-line suddenly, the rocket man tumbling as fingers of blood jetted from his chest. Then the blast drove spikes into his eardrums, the racket cleaving his brain, as he fell back, hauling the woman with him, fairly certain the warhead had impacted against the ceiling. True enough, judging the renewed fury of enemy fire, all the blast did was hurl yet more roiling smoke and dust to obscure the commandos. The woman began to scream hysterically as he held back on the assault rifle's trigger, spraying the corridor downrange, punching holes through the ballooning pall.

Something flashed up at him from beneath the smoke and lit the veil of his autofire. Bharjkhan was torn between the canisters flying down the corridor, spewing funnels of smoke, and the box that was suddenly glaring its red eye.

God had his answered his prayers! Where one box now worked...

He released the woman, shoving her away. It didn't matter now where she was as long as he took out as many of the enemy as possible. She was falling to the floor, shrieking in pure terror, when the cloud with its fiery bite of gas clawed into his eyes and nose, immolating senses. Somehow he clutched onto the box, his finger flying for the button when—

The body of one of his own men came crashing into his chest, hot liquid spattering eyes that were tearing rapidly to complete blindness.

Then Bharjkhan felt the first of many hammer blows from unyielding projectiles driving into his chest. He was pitching back to the roar of autofire, screaming in pain, then horror as he glimpsed the box sailing from his hand, swallowed up by the rushing clouds.

THE FIRST HUMAN BOMB blew a few seconds into their charge of the shopping complex for round two. Actually, Alvarado spotted two martyrs mummified around the torso in high-explosives, as they came darting out from behind the spread wings on either side of the twenty-foot marble Falcon statue, bellowing, "God is great!"

The lobby and the wide corridor leading to the pool were still under siege, about sixty yards to the southwest and east, as he heard autofire in both directions, the lag teams warring on to nail the last few standing threats. The running plan for the vanguard was shoot until the enemy dropped, trailer squads to secure evacuated turf, but keep on pushing.

No matter what.

The extremist human bombs began triggering assault rifles with ungainly one-handed sweeps of the wide no-man's land between the rows of glass-walled shops, other hooded shooters boiling out from the open doors to the restaurant, triggering weapons, wild men rushing for doom and damnation. Hostages were shuddering blurs in Alvarado's long view but racing down the other end, seizing the opportunity to save themselves best they could, when the SIU colonel dropped to one knee beside a statue of some naked goddess he didn't recognize nor much care about.

Zeno and his commandos were flying up into his peripheral vision, the Delta Force shooters seeking fire points in cramped alcoves or shop doorways, none of them needing orders to follow through. All of them cut loose on both sides with subgun fire, Alvarado thinking he spied the hand and lower arm of one walking human bomb erupting in a mist of red goo and gristle, when number two martyr blew.

Alvarado hit the deck, nearly kissing the goddess's feet as his lady savior took the brunt of the tidal wave of smoke, glass and other debris blowing over his position.

PADDING SWIFTLY BUT SILENTLY over carpet, the Executioner was homed in on the angry demands for silence and the sharp cries and pleading outbursts for release when the fanatic wheeled around the bend in the corridor. No solid plan of attack in mind other than hit and git and bulldoze through as many savages as he could, Bolan slammed the AK's stock squarely into the hooded face. As either luck or pure white-hot agony had it, the AK-74 slipped from the militant's hands on his way down to hammer the carpet, no reflexive warning shots triggered. Blood swam into the terrorist's mouth, threatening to suffocate him as Bolan pinned the savage with a knee to his chest, planted the AK's muzzle square between bugging eyes.

The corridor appeared empty for the moment, other than the sounds of terror filtering through the cracked doors to the suite immediately ahead. Combat senses told the Executioner they were alone with this next group of hostages and terrorists, the immediate vicinity in both directions free of visible opposition. Whatever was happening on the frontal assault by armed outside intervention, wherever hooded opposition walked, hunkered or hid, how many hostages and what booby traps he may or may not encounter, the soldier vowed to follow the terror trail, wherever it led.

Unless and until something more viable dropped into his lap.

Right then, the Executioner found he couldn't have asked for any better edge, given what he had in mind next, spotting the plastic cuffs jutted out of the fanatic's combat vest.

Harmon—or whatever his real name—flew past, AK-47 holding steady on the doors before he whipped into position on the far side. Settling into a crouch, he peered through the opening, mouthed it was clear.

Only both of them knew the enemy was somewhere down at the end of the foyer, judging distance to voices still barking for quiet.

"How many inside and where?" Bolan quietly asked his prisoner, menace in his voice.

The terrorist shook his head, coughing on blood, eyes burning with hate and defiance. He cursed Bolan in English.

Good enough.

Bolan plucked the cuffs, flipped him over and fastened his hands behind his back. He jacked the fanatic to his feet, held Harmon's eye and slowly whispered, "Follow my lead."

Harmon nodded his understanding.

Bolan tugged off the hood, the terrorist opening his mouth to shout when the soldier rammed enough of the fabric past his teeth so that it stayed wedged. He shoved him toward the doors, forced him to his knees. Harmon tensed to shoot, as Bolan listened to the voices. He figured thirty or so feet away, mentally gauging distance with sketches in mind of two suite foyers he'd so far seen, though nothing from there on was even remotely written in stone. Right now was a light-year leap, an eternity, if his play went to hell. Risky, damn right, considering innocent lives hung in the balance, but smart money told him the hostages—however many—were corralled somewhere in the living room.

There was no time to waste.

Quickly, setting down the AK, he pulled a grenade from his vest, armed it and shoved the sphere down the back of the fanatic's pants.

"Be silent or we will kill you all!"

"Mustafa! Where are you?"

Grabbing his human bulldozer by the shoulder and belt buckle, Bolan ran on a few feet, then hurled him through the doors. He was airborne and sailing down the foyer as the Executioner hauled in his assault rifle, spotted an armed gunner wheeling around the corner at the far end. The fanatic slammed to the floor, skidded on three or four feet, Bolan bolting to grab a corner as autofire ripped loose. The soldier's vanguard, he glimpsed on the fly, shuddered to his feet, absorbing several rounds from two of his savages in jihad, jerking and twitching, then he was blown to countless bits and pieces of shredded nothing.

TEAR GAS!

As if his entire living being wasn't dissected enough by the unholy clamor of autofire, endless screams and the cleaving from scalp to toes of shock waves from at least two massive explosions by last count, Ishtar Dharjab was forced to breathe in the scalding fumes of tear gas the enemy had dropped into the restaurant proper.

As he feared, the noxious clouds began to turn the tide of battle in favor of their enemies, commandos in protective masks and helmets puncturing the thick drifting palls in a lightning burst, splitting off to the sides after their initial charge down the foyer, tracking, firing. Subguns jumping in the enemy's black-gloved fists, at least four of his warriors, he spied were kicked off their feet where they reeled in the dense patches of smoke.

Dharjab had to think quickly, or go down in the mayhem, and he had no true wish to die. Martyrdom was meant for the lesser rank and rile. Commanders, by virtue of experience and wisdom, were deemed worthy of life beyond any battle, if only to continue jihad. And only a chosen few here, he knew, were aware of the planned escape route, which briefly begged the question as to why only the cell taking down the Presidential Suites had its own gas and masks in the first place. With the State Department official who was the big catch already in the bag, the rest of his brethren, he knew, were ordered to stand their ground and die as martyrs, kill as many infidels as possible in the process, and hopefully collapse the building.

Which begged another and even more insidious question beyond the fact none of them here were equipped with protective masks, though the answer was staring him right in the face, all around him with stuttering subguns, in truth, dropping his men like broken domino chips.

The sudden revelation that he, too, was meant to die, only served to inflame his own fear to clear the battleground, as the tumult seemed to shoot to another ear-shattering crescendo, so loud and piercing it seemed to swirl the acid vat in his clenched stomach at the merciless assault to his senses. Weapon in hand, Dharjab began charging for the double swing doors at the far end of the bar, bowling down three of four infidels who were spiraling in his path, torn as to which direction they should scatter. Three men and one woman rushed his way, blocking his flight. Holding back on the AK-47's trigger, he raked them in a long burst, kicking them off their feet, ragged sheets of blood flying toward the doors to his freedom.

Dharjab was leaping bodies, when he looked to the left, his ears catching the familiar war cry from one of his warriors. He saw the red light, flashing on the box clutched in the hand of his fellow holy fighter, Dharjab feeling his knees buckle at the sight. The martyr, he feared, was too far gone to hear him, much less care about an order to stop the madman's play, as he marched on, oblivious to all else, screaming at the top of his lungs. Dharjab considered shooting the man in the head, but the fool was then partially swallowed up inside a herd of fleeing infidels, a bull on a rampage, hostages bouncing off him like pinballs. There was enough C-4 primed to blow, he knew, to take out most, if not all the restaurant.

The martyr was close to fulfilling his death wish.

Dharjab gathered speed, ready to hurl his own scream of horror into the mix, then the world erupted into pure thunder and fire.

HARMON COULDN'T BELIEVE IT. He thought he knew the dirty business of black ops and hand-to-hand butchery, complete with every conceivable form of torture and degradation that could be heaped on a human being. He thought he'd seen every act of blood-letting in the trenches known to man and Satan, considered himself a pure killing machine.

But that was way back when.

Now he was stepping into a whole other dimension.

That doomed militant, festooned with blocks of what looked to be C4, bellowed some sort of war cry and blew up dozens of hostages in addition to several of his cohorts. It was an eyepopper for Harmon, beyond even his wildest comprehension and raw experience. The sheer horror of the scene would have left even the most hardened of combat juggernauts shaken.

The big guy was already charging down the foyer, low, and hugging the wall, assault rifle out and ready to slice and dice. Screams and bellowed threats rifled from around the corner. A dark hooded figure, jumpy AK in hand and flaming, lurched into view at the far end, and with human armor intact. Harmon figured he'd better do his part to hold up the charade. Mike the Stone Killer, he knew, would smell him out for the rat bastard he was, unless he dived right in, of course, zapping whatever extremist garbage was down there beyond all the smoke.

There was another brief staccato burst of autofire, accentuated by more shouts and shrieks, rounds punching through the swelling smoke balloon. Harmon bulled ahead, sticking to Mike's rear, just in case, spied half a black hood sheared away, a chunk of dark pulpy scalp taking to the air. The woman the terrorist had held, sporting a string bikini, wailed as she toppled back with the man's deadweight. A lightning check of the score so far, on the fly past two shredded slabs of outstretched meat, and Harmon figured four were down.

There was no time, he knew, to admire the big guy's action. It was scan and shoot, all the way into the living room and wherever else militant SOBs marked their turf. As the assault rifle blazed away in Mike's fists, the big guy grabbing immediate cover behind a floor-to-ceiling statue of Earth now dappled with blood and ragged shreds of flesh, Harmon hit a crouch at the end of the foyer. He wasn't looking to play hero, but he knew the big guy was of a different mind, light-years, from any self-serving agenda. If he didn't know better, Harmon figured the guy actually cared whether or not innocent hostages lived or died, that the big hitter was now on a personal crusade to save life while he evened up the score. Truth was, Harmon would have preferred to just hole up with the others, wait for the commando cavalry to set them truly free.

Now this!

He was taking fire, damn it to hell, the edge of the wall scourged by rounds, ten inches or so above his head, a few more near misses threatening to steal his dreams. The suite, he believed, was billed the Stargazer, if he recalled his perusal of the Presidential abodes correctly. The walls of the living room bubbled out and around, like three-quarters of a flying saucer, the walls silver, mirrored in spots. There were hanging stars, moons, planets beneath a skylight frescoed with solar systems and other deep space gases and phenomenon over a hot tub roomy enough for a party of twelve or more. Two giant plasma TVs hung from the lunar-pocked ceiling from wires invisible to the naked eye.

Harmon cursed his sudden distraction. He wasn't there to stargaze either, though the four or five scantily clad Nordic playthings hitting the plush white carpet between the crescent moon-shaped couches snagged an admiring eye for a brief second. The three men they were partying with either had good sense or were just too damned scared as they nosedived for cover. That opened up a clean line of fire on four hooded specters downrange, who were shooting and screaming like there was no tomorrow.

There wasn't.

It became one big sweet shooting gallery in the next instant.

One of the militants was already twitching on his back, courtesy of a burst of rounds from Mike's AK-47. Harmon threw in a long sweeping afterburner of autofire. Numbers two and three militants were bellowing how great was Allah, triggering spray and pray, as Harmon converged with Mike's blistering hose of the lead clamp. Dust, glass and plaster hurled a meteor shower over number four as he began taking rocket shots from Mike, Fanatics two and three collapsing to mashed and bloody heaps. Harmon hit martyr four with his own scythe of lead skewers, the militant hammering the skylight above with a long burst as he was pounded back.

"Watch the door!"

"No problem," Harmon growled, more to himself than anybody else since Mike was already heading out to check on the living and the dead.

KATERINA MUSCOVKY WANTED to believe the worst of it was over, but she wasn't so sure.

Not when she heard what sounded like distant sonic booms, the floor beneath her feet trembling in brief spasms of seismic ripples. Those were explosions, she was certain, and the others became alarmed at what she guessed was pitched warfare underway somewhere in the hotel.

They were gathered in the master bedroom, but none of the former hostages looked too eager to venture beyond the open doors where the group leader—another Mike—was armed and watching for any return by the terrorists. Some of them, mostly the women, sat on the bed or one of two large divans, drinks and smokes in hand. Others wandered around, wringing hands, still terrified, and who could blame them? Some of them whined about this and that, helping themselves to the wet bar like the movie star and his agent. Cameron was working hard, she assumed, to regain the image of celluloid courage he had so miserably fallen short of before a live audience. The man in the white jacket and his three comrades again began to angrily demand that Mike cut them loose, let them leave, bellowing now near the door. Moments ago she recalled he seemed to think about it, but there was something about them he didn't seem to trust. They reminded her of Dmitri, slick and hard, full of themselves, malice in the eyes, concerned only about saving face at the moment. On the flip side in every respect, the family man, she knew, had been granted an assault rifle, Mike having briefly shown him the basics. The man was sitting now in the far corner with his wife and children. Muscovky gave him due credit for courage and the willingness to stand and protect his own blood, even if it cost him his life. He might look ordinary on the surface, but here and now he was the male lion defending his pride, all heart, all guts. Yes, he was afraid—and only an arrogant fool or psychopath wouldn't be under these circumstances—but he had freely accepted the role thrust upon him by fate.

Alone in a leather recliner near a bay window overlooking the beach, she determined to ignore all of them, as her thoughts locked back onto her single greatest fear. Despite his solemn vow before leaving…

He would return, she prayed, he had to, after all they'd been through together, but when? Or what if…

Suddenly she felt terribly alone. She wondered—afraid—

if he was hurt, and silently cursed the fact he had deemed it fit to march out, armed to the teeth, leave her alone, then realized she was being selfish. She was confident, nonetheless, if there was a new threat at least the designated group leader had the courage and the skill to defend them. The more she thought about it the more both Mikes bore some similarity. Not so much in physical terms, but the way they carried themselves, quiet, confident they could handle the gravest of situations—and had proved they could. Beyond that, they weren't about themselves, their survival, nor wishing to cling solely to whatever their claim and stature on life. Rather, they valued the lives of the innocent and defenseless, no matter how insufferable, weak or undeserving the life to be saved.

Muscovky shot a brief look toward the paunchy man in the expensive silk jacket and slacks, hunched in another deep corner. Keeping his distance from the others, he was lost in his own world of what looked like private grief, as she noted some vague resemblance to the priest, thinking back that the man had called him "brother," but she couldn't be certain what she'd heard before and during…

She shuddered, sick to her stomach when she remembered. The image of the priest's murder was branded into her mind's eye, leaving her to briefly wonder if she would ever forget the horror, what nightmares she would endure in the future, assuming she survived beyond this room. Now that she thought about it, though, it struck her that he had sacrificed his own life to buy time for the rest of them—and she suspected the gruesome execution had given Mike another reason to go to hunt down terrorists who might be lurking the top floor.

Mike Cooper.

Oh, and he was far more, she knew, than he originally claimed, wondering if she could trust her own instincts at all about men after what she'd seen. That he had killed so quickly and with no seeming effort, told her she hadn't known the real man at all. She should be bothered by how he could so easily dispense death, cold, efficient and remorseless, as if it was something he did all the time like most people went to an office job. Then again, had he not acted when he did, one or more of them may have been chosen for execution next. Truth be told, she was reasonably sure he had been searching for a way to escape and fight back since he'd come to and found how desperate their situation was. Whatever his background, she owed and respected him.

She saw the other Mike step into the bedroom. Clearly exasperated with the four who reminded her of Dmitri he cut them loose, but kept the assault rifle aimed in their vicinity. They began growling among themselves in a language she recognized as Serbo-Croatian, their women rushing to them. They left as a group, but no one else appeared interested to follow their lead.

"You want a drink?"

She knew who it was before she turned toward the wet bar, felt the sides of her mouth beginning to tighten into a scowl. The Hollywood Hero was holding up an empty glass and a bottle, pasting on what he hoped, she was sure, was an inviting smile, geared up to lay on the charm. She supposed she could forgive him his pathetic display, the self-serving defiance, if it had not led to the murder of the priest. Briefly, she wondered if they were all like him in Hollywood, so despicably narcissistic, their own lives and lifestyles of wealth and stardom they were prepared to cling to it all, no matter what, and even if that meant someone else had to suffer or die in their place. Sadly, she supposed their narrow superficial world and the myopic view they held of the rest of the human race rivaled the one she had left behind.

She looked at Cameron, saw his eyes light up, this clown actually thinking he had a shot. Before the booze kicked in, he had been sulking around, grumbling and cursing his agent, circumstance, life in general, scrambling already, from what little she'd overheard, to spin the right amount of damage control in order to keep his world from becoming unraveled by the truth. She suspected once news of the real Bret Cameron reached the tabloids his troubles had only just begun. Fool that he was, he didn't know it yet.

"I'll pass," she told him.

"Hey, why not? We've got some time to kill here…"

She put the right amount of ice in her eyes and voice. "I will tell you once more. No. Do not ask me again."

He was sputtering as she turned away, leaving him to whatever his muttered response.

She clung to the hope that Mike Cooper would return to her soon, safe and unharmed.

SITTING STILL, WAITING FOR rescue, was never an option. Katerina Muscovsky would keep, Bolan knew. From his standpoint, the only safe assurance to keep from falling under another terrorist threat was to march out of the suite, hunt them down to extermination before more trouble came to them.

That, and delivering a blood debt. Bolan could be reasonably sure vengeance would have been unacceptable to the priest—and to some extent he could understand and respect that—but only in a perfect world could he find himself willing to love his enemies.

In a perfect world, he knew there would be no reason for his War Everlasting to exist.

Fresh cannibals were in the vicinity beyond the stairwell door leading to the eleventh floor of suites. His AK-47 charged with a fresh 30-round banana clip, Bolan zeroed in on the muffled growls and shouts in the corridor, off to his right. He took a moment on the way down to listen to the stairwells and platforms directly below. No threat down there, he determined, at least for the immediate present, but running blind as he was, he maintained vigilance. The enemy could pop up anytime, anywhere.

Warrior logic dictated the roof had been swept clean of the big guns and opposition. The strike force would come at the enemy, from top down, bottom up, taking them down as they showed, squeezing them toward the middle of the complex.

Bolan thus knew his own time to snuff the enemy and save hostages on his front was running out.

As for Harmon's role, Bolan—rolling up to the door, searching the jamb for wires or other booby traps but finding no telltale signs of a threat—wasn't sure where the man stood. He seemed to be hanging back, with no sense of dire urgency to go the distance against armed opposition.

The big question left begging an answer was why Harmon had a pistol on his person in the first place, his hands free the whole time where it sure as hell seemed the militants had bound anyone they sensed a menace. An enigma, and one Bolan intended to solve at some future point. Harmon was an extra gun, whatever the case, but the soldier didn't trust his back to the man any longer than necessary to advance to the next stage.

The Executioner paused at the door, listening as the angry conversation began to drift farther away. "You been on this floor?"

Harmon bunched up behind Bolan's back. "No. Why would I?"

"Anything I need to know?"

"Such as?"

"If you are what I think, then maybe you know what this is all about and who's leading this pack of savages."

"Let's just say, Mike, that's knowledge best left alone for the time being."

"Meaning you'd have to kill me if you told me?"

Harmon chuckled. "Remember what you said about trust?"

Bolan's mental radar blipped louder about the guy, but he didn't push it. "You take my six—to the left—and anything on up to my ten."

"It's your party, big guy."

Bolan showed Harmon a steely eye. "Hey. This isn't some reality TV nonsense."

"I can dig it. Your six to ten, I got it."

Taking a deep breath, Bolan threw the door open. Two steps into the corridor, he read the situation, his AK up and tracking. Four extremists were in the process of marching away when they sensed the threat to their rear. There was a glass barrier to Bolan's left wing, a health spa, he realized as he took up slack on the AK's trigger. Two more fanatics appeared, shoving their human shields toward the door ahead of the treadmills when autofire roared in Bolan's ear. One of the hardmen in the spa was taking hits from Harmon behind the tumbling sheets of glass, as the Executioner caressed the trigger, riding out precise double-taps, taking out fanatics as they released their hostages. Extremists three and four on either flank finished their turn just in time to catch full-auto bursts in the chest, Bolan driving them back and down to boneless heaps, the captives—a man and a woman—already in nosedive for the carpet. The Executioner was swinging the AK toward the spa, scanning the deep interior with its aerobics and weight machines, just as Harmon's second tag dropped onto a treadmill.

Clear, it looked, but Bolan waved for Harmon to check the spa anyway, then searched the corridor in both directions, the racket of screams melding with the sudden screech of a fire alarm. He felt the hair rise on his nape, looking back at the door, sixth sense warning him their rear wasn't covered.

The overhead sprinklers hissed on, as the Executioner raced back for the door, straining to hear through the ringing in his ears. AK up and ready, he heard shouts in Arabic, maybe three or four voices, militants coming up the stairwell.

Grasping the doorknob, he twisted, flung the door open. Glancing up, finding the stairs clear, he heard them closing, bounding hard up the steps. Two, then three hooded terrorists whipped around the corner post, wild eyes raw with hate and furious determination spotting him, their assault rifles greeting his own burst. Ricochets zoomed from the metal post, stone shrapnel blasting from the wall behind the fanatics, as they fell back from the soldier's blazing tempest. They were still shouting, regrouping when the soldier filled his hands with the RPG-7. If they had hostages he would have heard the usual pleas or cries. They were moving way too fast to concern themselves with the luggage of human shields.

Two or three came back firing around the post when the Executioner loosed the warhead and blew their twisted vision all to hell.

**17**

Colonel Sebastian Alvarado didn't need to barge into the Grand Ballroom on the third floor behind the Delta Force SIU squad to know it was a wall-to-wall charnel house. One suicidal madman he knew of had already blasted through those hostages in there. How many body bags, he wondered, and just for this slaughterhouse alone? How many more wounded, or hideously maimed and scarred for life? Then there were six KIAs and four hanging on by the most slender of threads, an even split between SIU and Delta Force the last he heard from the head medic. How many more good men would forfeit their lives before the last rat was flushed out and exterminated?

And it wasn't over yet, not by a long shot.

Hanging back for the sitreps, he listened to the first reports of new additional action underway in other areas of the hotel, as squads hit the stairwells, taking back the hotel, floor by floor, suite by suite. Elevators had been blown, leaving behind gaping craters, with broken bodies strewn in corridors demolished so thoroughly there was no telling who was who, which body part belonged where. Hostages were still held by the enemy in several suites on the fifth, seventh and ninth floors, with suicidal maniacs roving hallways, gunning down anything that moved. And his handheld unit, fixed to his belt, crackled on with the angry voice of Commander Zeno tracking down and sifting through each additional mess and horror, barking out the new round of orders down the line.

Alvarado shed his mask and hung it on his belt, as the tear gas dissipated and withering bursts of weapons fire and screams of terror kept flaying the air. Out of nowhere, amid all the pandemonium, he somehow caught a groan followed by a vicious curse from a few feet to his right. Weapon tracking the source of pain, he turned toward a litter of dead bodies.

There, stretched out before him, was a hooded human serpent, blood pumping out of shoulder and upper chest wounds, one of the man's legs bent at an angle, broken somehow by the trampling herds of his victims. Even as death reached out for the militant, Alvarado found the slitted eyes inside the hood burned his way with hate and defiance. Something that felt like an ice-cold veil fell over the colonel, head to foot. Then he marched up to the wounded terrorist sprawled on the carpet, the snake eyes flickering in a last desperate search for a weapon. As the racket of weapons fire suddenly erupted inside the ballroom, Alvarado drilled a 3-round burst into the terrorist's chest, point-blank, then pumped in a few more slugs for the hell of it. Maybe God would have mercy on the evil bastard's soul, he thought, but given what he saw strewed all around, the magnitude of the atrocity and suffering and death the enemy had inflicted from the lobby on up, he somehow seriously doubted it.

Alvarado reckoned the terrorist and his ilk had special hot seats reserved all for them in the deeper regions of Hell.

He was forced to leave grisly mop-up to the combined commando force, as his squad leader began patching through with a sitreps over the com link. Angry stare locked on the open doors to the murder vault, he backstepped, subgun fanning the madness of guests screaming and fleeing in both ways down the corridor as they shuffled or bolted from the dark smoky maw to the Ballroom.

The security-utility labyrinth was secured, he was informed first off, the fire alarms and water sprinklers now shutting down to alleviate some of the team's own confusion and obscured vision in the chaos of running battle. When Alvarado heard at what cost to innocent life the C and C room was taken back, he choked down another rising fist of hot fury. Then he heard how thoroughly the fanatics had mined the underground complex, what was the base of twelve stories, he knew. The exact poundage had yet to be determined, but the initial ballpark figure was four digits easy, which, he guessed, would reach into the tons when all was counted and the smoke of battle finally cleared. There were enough explosives at first look, he was told, that the jihadists might have blasted out enough of the foundation to cause the hotel to crash to the ground.

"Mother of God," he muttered to himself, but a faint voice somewhere in the cavities of dark thought informed him that the operation had staved off a major catastrophe and even more incalculable loss to life.

So far.

Alvarado then heard from his team leader in the security command center, wondering at the strange note in his voice as he was told, "Sir, we have an ongoing combat situation on the ninth floor. Two men, who appear to be civilians, are armed, and they just killed three hostiles…"

Alvarado listened with one ear to the incredible report. Whomever they were, they had vanished from camera range, as he gathered from the play-by-play from his team leader. Alvarado wondered. Descend to the next level and carry on their own private war? The next few seconds seemed to freeze all sound and movement around him, as Alvarado heard his hand-held unit rage with the voice of Zeno and that of another man he didn't recognize, his attention suddenly torn between both transmissions.

"I'm Mike Cooper. I'm with the United States Department of Justice. Check it."

"Like I have the time," Zeno growled. "You listen to me! I don't give a damn if you are the avenging angel of death sent by the Almighty Himself, you are interfering with—"

The guy calling himself Mike Cooper went on as if Zeno didn't exist, weapons fire rattling over the transmission. "There are hostages in the Presidential Suites on the top floor. If you have men coming down from the roof you are to alert them—"

Alvarado keyed his com link. "BackSurge Leader. Confirm again. Two men who appear to be civilians but who are armed and last seen on the ninth floor, and give me a present location ASAP."

"Yes, sir. Repeat—two men. Civilian dress, last seen… Sir! They are now on the eighth floor. Both still armed and closing now in the direction of a group of what looks four, no five hostiles. Hostiles, sir, are on the move in a south vector, and holding a group of hostages, I count five civilians."

Alvarado heard Zeno squawking, but Mike Cooper, he suspected, was already gone. A second later, that was confirmed as BackSurge Leader informed him the two civilians were now engaging the enemy. What the hell was going on? Alvarado thought.

The commanding tone in Mike Cooper's tone told Avarado he was a take charge guy. The colonel decided he needed to scale the steps fast to lend a helping or bailing hand, as yet another caldron of blood and madness appeared about to bubble over.

COMBAT INSTINCTS TOLD Harmon the eighth floor was where it would end, one way or another. The moment to cut and run—meaning drill Mike the Stone Killer with an AK stitching up the back—had come and gone at the spa.

Following the blue-eyed man's RPG shellacking of a few more militant jackals on the stairwell, where they began their descent for what he knew would prove the bowels of Hell, Mike seemed to have grown eyes in the back of his head, but Harmon wasn't surprised the guy didn't trust him. In his place, he would have felt the same way.

Trust no one.

There had been about a two minute lull in the frenzied action down the stairs, time enough for Harmon to try to chart a new course. But a quick vanishing act was looking more unlikely with each yard, each kill, as Big Mike, he recalled, waxed three more jihadists on the ninth floor, the unlucky trio caught in a wrestling act with a few more hostages, now set free.

It had been far from easy so far, but any more coasting from there on was a dead man's hope.

The big guy had to have sensed the hook coming himself, as the strike force began announcing its presence in the lower floors. Each new round of weapons fire that echoed up and down the stairwell seemed to lend the big crusader new angry energy to pick up the pace.

Like now.

Two more extremists were down and twitching out from Mike's last lightning rod of AK fire, crimson streaks and ragged bits of flesh staining the wall above the latest sorry sacks, but Harmon was braced for another deadly surprise in the coming heartbeats. Assault rifle up and out, he was swinging around a statue of some Roman soldier when Mike raced ahead for the closest point of cover. Harmon watched the man blur behind another sculpted warrior, this one with sword high in the air and saddled on a rising stallion, the guy locking those grim death sights on the five armed terrorists heading for what looked like some tropical lover's garden. They had hostages, five to be exact, all of them held out front, living shields, leaving the backs of the extremists exposed. Without warning, two of the male captives turned on the closest militants, spurred on by either courage born of hope on the way or pure blind panic.

It really didn't matter, but it gave Mike all the opening he needed.

Whether it was dumb luck, or somehow instinctively already knowing each other's moves, Harmon began his line of fire on the left wing, while his one-man wrecking crew drilled the first two militants to the far right. Three of the Muslim gunners took hits to the lower back, then ribs, drilled into half-spins but firing on with wild jerky sweeps of autofire. Harmon glimpsed number four lunging to grab a human shield. No such luck. The militant fulfilled his death wish but only after a few brief seconds of agony, as Mike chopped him down at the knees, then dealt the militant a burst to the head.

Harmon took out number five, slamming him back with an extended salvo to the torso and into the waiting arms of some prehistoric-looking jungle foliage, where he plunged out of sight. Hostages were hitting the deck, all flailing arms and screams.

The CIA spook suddenly felt the hackles bristling on the back of his neck. Hostages, he saw, shimmied to their feet, but the big guy warned them to stay down, clearly sensing something wrong himself. Autofire reverberated from several directions, the stink of smoke, cordite and blood swimming into Harmon's nose, the sum total of distant battle and death in his face seeming to render some invisible but menacing presence he couldn't determine. He could feel it in the air, guts knotting up, battle instincts shrieking that it was all about to hit the fan again and one of them was set to get zapped up the creek without a paddle.

Where? How many?

Venturing two steps forward, Harmon flickered his eyes from the doors ahead of the big guy, who was sweeping the vicinity, twelve to six and back, with his assault rifle. Two rooms up, on each side, maybe a hundred feet or so before they reached the hostages…

And then it all plunged to hell.

The martyr came flying out from behind door number two to Mike's twelve o'clock. There was no mistaking the torso wraps for what they were, or the box in his hand as he squeezed off a one-handed AK burst in the big guy's direction. Harmon wheeled into a one-eighty, bolting for cover around the corner beyond the statue, leaving the big guy to fend for himself. It was time to save his own skin with no looking back, as he suspected Mike's number had finally come up.

But he needed more breathing room, a little more clearance from ground zero himself!

Harmon was four steps and racing, cursing his rotten luck, then launched himself off his feet as the anticipated sonic boom erupted.

"That him?"

"Yes, sir, that would be him."

By all rights, Bolan knew he had no business being alive. Had he not thrown himself through the partly opened door to the suite when he did, he would have been tucked inside one of the many black body bags he found laid out in the front parking lot of the hotel. Even still, the hammering shock waves from the suicide blast had done a punishing number on him. According to the medic who had just finished stitching up the deepest of several gashes on his scalp and forehead, he'd been unconscious for well over sixty minutes—and that didn't include whatever missing time it took for Spanish commandos to discover his body buried beneath all the rubble dropped over him by the martyr's blast. That piece of news came from a Lieutenant Morado of the Special Intervention Unit who was standing by when the soldier came around in the emergency medical vehicle. Had it not been for other victims with more serious injuries that required immediate attention, Bolan assumed he would have landed in the closest hospital. In limbo, out of the loop.

Apparently, his private war had been caught on security cameras, and he had more than piqued the interest of one Colonel Alvarado. Some thirty minutes earlier, Bolan had dispatched the lieutenant to hunt down the colonel, after telling him who and what he was, running down a brief list of his own demands, which included a report on Katerina Muscovky and the other hostages he'd left behind.

The Executioner spotted a tall lean man in black fatigues, brandishing a subgun, stride away from Morado. Waiting for who he assumed was Colonel Alvarado to bridge the gap, Bolan took in the pandemonium. He found nothing short of a war zone as he hopped out of the back of the medic wagon, waving off the Spanish doctor's insistence he needed to lay down, something about concussion, the possibility of internal injuries, bleeding and such.

The soldier supposed he had lived through worse, but he couldn't quite remember when he'd walked through the kind of hell zone he now recalled leaving behind. He did, in fact, feel more than a little shaky as he sucked in and exhaled several deep slow breaths.

Forget about himself. There were plenty of others far worse off. Choppers roved the skies, he saw, scouring the hotel, vicinity and rooftop with searchlights. Commandos and medics were racing all over the lot, too many gurneys to count wheeled to medic wagons, as fire vehicles and more EMVs barreled past the wide-open entrance gate. Charred and smoking skeletons of vehicles and scattered wreckage at the deep east end didn't escape Bolan's eye either, telling him the war inside had found its way beyond this hell's inner sanctum.

But he was alive, and so was Muscovky, as far as he knew, the soldier waiting now, hoping for confirmation she was breathing and in one piece.

How many innocents, though, had perished here this night of murder and fanatic insanity? he wondered, anger slicing through the sludge in heavy, sore limbs, adrenaline helping to fuel a second wind. Was every last savage, in fact, dead or captured? In all the mayhem and wanton butchery, factoring in the vast expanse of the complex, and he had to suspect a few of the cannibals somehow managed to escape ultimate justice. When considering the lightning efficiency with which they had seized the hotel, his gut told him the enemy vipers had more than a little inside help. Perhaps to slither out, as much as to get in and locked on.

So many questions. So many dead and wounded.

And where did it—he—go from there?

"I am Colonel Alvarado."

Bolan waited for the man to continue, but Alvarado simply stood his ground, the Spanish commando leader peering into the soldier's eyes, wondering or maybe deciding something.

Alvarado handed Bolan his briefcase and duffel. "Your weapons and satellite phone have not been touched. I appreciate you trusting Lieutenant Morado enough to give him the correct numbers to the lock."

Bolan nodded. "And the hostages, the woman I left behind?"

"Safe and unharmed, the last I was informed. Whether they wish to or not, they will be examined whenever our doctors can get to them, then they will be briefly detained and questioned."

"Questioned?"

"I am not at liberty to discuss any more details at this time. It will take days, perhaps months, as I am sure you would understand, for any conclusions about what happened here…well, suffice it to say there will be an ongoing investigation."

"Implying whoever was responsible for this hell on Earth had a few doors opened for them to step on in and set up shop." When it was clear Alvarado wasn't about to volunteer any information, Bolan asked, "When can I see the woman?"

"I cannot be precise on the time."

"You do realize, Colonel, that I am a special agent with the United States Department of Justice? That your cooperation or lack of will not go unnoticed?" Bolan said, playing the rare political card.

"Yes, I do, indeed. And I am well aware of all the nasty international ramifications of this disaster. My seeming lack of cooperation has more to do with, well, orders from my own superiors. However, I have been in touch with the American Embassy where I was given instructions by them through your own superior."

So Brognola knew, Bolan thought. The big Fed's considerable clout, which sometimes required the backing of the

President of the United States, had smoothed choppy waters, at least for the moment.

Alvarado looked set to scowl but checked the expression. "If you were not cleared and I did not believe you were a man of some authority to be reckoned with I would not have returned those weapons."

"So, that's that? I'm free to go?"

"That would depend on you."

Alvarado looked up, Bolan turning and spotting the Black Hawk as it descended. As the gunship touched down a few yards away, the soldier looked into the open fuselage.

"You look like about two months' worth of stepped-on crap, Special Agent Cooper."

Bolan felt a sudden urge to wipe the grin off that face. However, he let Harmon have his chuckle, the man looming in the hatch, donned in fresh black fatigues, an HK subgun hung over a shoulder. The combat vest, Bolan noted, was stuffed to the gills with spare clips, grenades, a Beretta 92-F in shoulder holster replacing the Walther Harmon had used back at the suite.

Loaded for war.

To say it all reeked to hell…

"Why don't we get you cleaned up?" Harmon shouted. "Unless, that is, you'd rather stay here with your girlfriend. Or maybe you want a shot to go after the bastards behind this operation?"

**18**

In due time action betrayed the heart. There really was no such creature as hidden motive. The very nature of deceit demanded it reveal itself to the light of truth, if only out of pride where it believed itself smarter, better, more deserving.

Working off that tried and proved bottom line, Bolan determined not to drop his guard one nanosecond against Harmon. The guy was dirty. The soldier just didn't know how deep the stain, how far his corruption spread, and who else had been snared, willingly or not, by whatever his black bag of tricks.

At what he suspected was a CIA safe house north of Barcelona, Bolan had changed into a formfitting blacksuit, combat vest, webbing, then weapons from Harmon's personal and extensive cache in the cellar, the hardware getting a thorough strip and check. Standard side arms were now stowed in holsters, Ka-Bar fighting knife tucked in shin leather. To beef up the killing power, the Executioner had claimed an M-16 M-203 combo, spare clips and a mix of 40 mm grenades, enough to tackle whatever Harmon was about to dump on the table, which, so far, was little more info than scraps. A nylon war bag on the back seat of the black GMC was fat with two LAWs, one Uzi submachine gun, an RPG-7 and backup spares in mags and warheads, just in case Bolan needed extra boost to tackle as yet undetermined opposition and numbers. The portable handheld satellite unit was now clipped to his belt, but Bolan had not yet been able to steal enough time away from Harmon to touch base with Brognola.

The Executioner was flying solo, without much aid and assistance from the Farm. It was his game, he determined, to win or lose, and he was prepared to go the full distance with Harmon, and deal with any treachery or savagery. From there on it was a most deadly game of shadows within shadows, which the Executioner was all too grimly familiar with. And he could play it with the best—or the worst—of the rotten bunch.

Bolan sensed Harmon drilling steel bits into the side of his head. The black op was manning the wheel, as Bolan watched the dark night pass by, leaving Harmon to his thoughts and schemes as to maybe how he'd start the overdue briefing. The Stony Man warrior figured they were now a good twenty miles due northwest of the outer Barcelona suburbs, forging into Basque Country, the rugged hilly landscape dotted here and there with small villages and hamlets. It was the sorcerer's hour, well into early morning, and only a few lights shone from the hamlet of San Juan, as the name of the village was posted by the roadside sign. They passed a small church on a hill, Bolan mentally marking the giant crucifix, then took the left bend in a fork of dirt trails.

"You knew all along, didn't you," Bolan stated.

Harmon chuckled. "That it was the world's most wanted terrorist scumbag, the one and only Akhmadah al-Hamquadra who had us all by the short hairs back in that suite? No, I didn't, not until I saw the eyes. It was a scar on the right hand, shaped kind of like a serpent's tongue, that finally gave him away. There's none like that it our side knows of, and it's better than DNA, I'm thinking, when his ass is finally in the bag. I know, you've got a million and one questions."

Bolan did, but decided to let the hand of Fate guide him to the answers. Or, for the present, to allow Harmon to talk himself into a pit.

"Twenty million, U.S.," Harmon went on, "is on al-Hamquadra's scalp. That's a lot of cash for the guy or guys with a big enough pair to collect on." Harmon paused, glancing at Bolan, as if waiting on him to respond. "We had him bouncing all over Iraq for about two years and change, but couldn't peg him down. What with all his militant insurgents, the kind of cash he spread around, Iraqi cops on his payroll, too, all the safehouses at his ready convenience. I figure you know the deal, being with the Justice Department and all, how some snakes seem to always slide on and just when you think you got them by the tail. Forget the general public. There's a whole lot going on over there that doesn't even reach the eyes and ears of the almighty Central Command."

"Uh-huh. And he kidnapped anybody he branded on the wrong side of the former regime or the insurgent movement. He's believed to have the blood of more than thirty executions on his hands personally. A lot of them on tape. When he abducted then beheaded two American Marines and one embedded journalist, the CIA put this big bounty on his head, pretty much scratching off the 'or alive.' He must have decided things were a little too hot, being as he seems to have just vanished off the face of Iraq, or the planet for that matter, the last year or so," the Executioner growled.

Harmon went on as if he hadn't heard Bolan. "The former Syrian intelligence chief of operations funneled a lot of the ordnance into Iraq that was used to pile up the body count of Coalition Forces and everyday citizens and Iraqi police trainees. After about a hundred car bombs, we gave up keeping count how many he claimed responsibility for. He's a wholesale terror merchant, but Iraq's not his only store in that part of the world. Weapons. Cash to finance various operations. Recruiter of young jihadists. Builds training camps. Has close ties to a few Saudis with oil money by the tons, and is believed to have the ear and full blessing of bin Laden, and maybe, from what we hear, a direct line to the guy and a few others we missed in Afghanistan, translation being he may know the whereabouts on top tier wolves."

"If that's true, then he'd be worth more alive."

"You'd think—and it is true, pal—but that's not the way it works sometimes in black ops. Word is al-Hamquadra's in the process of brokering a deal with the North Koreans for a suitcase nuke or two, and some bio-horror not even the think tanks and war planners on our side want to contemplate. This guy is better off dead, trust me. We had him under surveillance, or thought we did, in Cairo right before the operation to take the hotel. That's been the problem. We get close, and he's like that wisp of smoke blown away by a strong wind."

"I bet you're going to tell me he managed to slip the net tonight."

"All the way back to his hole in North Africa is my best educated guess."

"And you know all this how?"

Harmon cut a mean smile. "I've been wondering when you'd start hurling some hardball questions. First, there's a State Department big shot by the name of James Talliman. His speciality is gathering intelligence on terrorist operations that may be in the works against our embassies, diplomats and such who might be in the crosshairs. Talliman came to Barcelona to dump off classified intel to the jihad side, big-time ops that would have either cornered Mr. Twenty Million Price tag or shut down about twenty-plus major terror cells and their ongoing operations clear around the globe. Probably both. We're talking all top tier operators Uncle Sam had under the magnifying glass and were ready to burn down. I managed to maneuver Talliman to the hotel at the last minute before I myself was bagged by al-Hamquadra's goons on the top floor."

"I had men on Talliman at one of the hotel's restaurants. Al-Hamquadra's cronies removed him from the other hostages after the takedown. He's in the wind, along with al-Hamquadra. The hotel may be back under the control of the good guys, albeit loosely, but it'll take the Spanish SIU and our own Delta shooters who were part of the strike force days, even weeks before they sort out and kick through all the mess and bodies and body parts back there. First casualty reports, I'm hearing anywhere from four to seven hundred, and that's covering a broad range of victims from a lot of countries that are going to want answers or heads rolling. While the strike force digs through the rubble trying to figure out who's who and what's what—and God only knows the international political warring that's about to cream Spain, cuffing every pair of good operator hands that can do the dirty work—I've got concrete intel on our boy. Uh-huh. And thus our problem. Seems the bad guys took a boat from one of the marinas out back, about two blocks north up the beach from the hotel. A couple of local dockhands we believe were recruited specifically for the operation were found shot dead on the wharf about the time you were getting your head stitched up. Yeah. The top tier never intended to go down with the ship once they nabbed Talliman."

Assume he was getting, at best, a string of half-truths, Bolan had to suspect the top-tier operators were right then being watched from space or monitored from fifty thousand feet up by recon birds or both. "And al-Hamquadra is right now sailing across the Mediterannean?"

Harmon shrugged. "That, or he and however many others slipped away when it got too hot were picked up by chopper."

Bolan considered what Harmon was—or wasn't—telling him. "I don't have a map handy, but the quickest and straightest line to refuge would be…"

"Algeria."

A few moments of silence passed. Bolan did not want to dwell on all the grim possibilities, that he was being led into the next phase for reasons only time would reveal. The dirt track grew narrow enough with inches to spare, tree branches and brush scraping the GMC's sides. Headlights pierced the pitched blackness, the trail arrow straight, but Bolan only found more of the same wooded gauntlet waiting in the distance.

"Why me, Harmon?"

"Why you, what?"

"It sounds like you've got it all figured out."

"Furthest thing from the truth. If you're asking why I picked you to hop on board, let's just say I liked your moves tonight," the covert agent told him.

Which meant, Bolan knew, nothing, and something else altogether. "You need an extra gun."

"What's about to happen is a small covert op. I have been given the reins, the green light, from where and from whom doesn't concern you. And, yeah, I could use a shooter with your obvious talent, since my own team is right now four operatives. All of whom will be on the ground just after sunrise down there."

Bolan's gut kept clenching tighter, with mental radar blipping louder the more Harmon talked. "Meaning you don't have the numbers crunched on the other end in Algeria?"

"Meaning I have some clues, but I'm going to need to spend the better part of the coming day piecing together the finer details before the two of us set sail. That is, if you decide you're up to the job," Harmon drawled.

Bolan let the dig slide. "These details of yours better be more than just fine. You realize you're talking about infiltrating one of the most murderous countries on the planet? Where the Armed Islamic Group, the Islamic Salvation Front and about twenty other splinter groups have all issued fatwas, and against their own government and military?"

Harmon chuckled. "And all that is you telling me you don't think I got the get up and go to tackle the job." He paused, glancing at Bolan, then went on, "Depending on who you talk to—State Department, various security firms that contract themselves out to foreign oil companies, the CIA, any number of globe-trotting journalists—the country's considered about neck and neck with Chechnya as the number one bad guy hellhole on Earth. The fundamentalists down there kill teachers and burn down schools with children still in them. I've seen them hang up old men and women and slit their throats like hogs on a spit for no damn good reason I could see, while army helicopters look on during a smoke break." Harmon paused for a moment, then quickly said, "I know the score. There was a few years back I practically lived there, pal."

Why did that make him a little extra nervous? Bolan wondered. "I suppose with all this hands-on knowledge you've got a master plan? One that includes rapid exfiltration?"

"How about I get to all that once we're in the air? Right now, we're going to meet one of the guests you might recall from our little soiree back in the suite. A fat guy in a white suit who was making a bunch of noise the whole time about wringing some necks?"

Bolan remembered, and had a good suspicion who the party in question was.

"You being with the Justice Department, which is in charge of the FBI, I'm assuming you've heard of Dragovan 'Drago' Vikholic?"

"Indicted Serb war criminal. Ran Belagorja, a death camp where he tried his best to incinerate the Muslim population. The CIA isn't sure how many thousands Vikholic had put in his ovens, burned alive, I might add."

"Sounds to me like I should be surprised you didn't just walk up to the man and put one between his eyes."

"I was a little busy at the time," Bolan replied.

"Good thing for him. Anything else I need to know about this kick-ass attitude I'm picking up?"

"Regarding Vikholic, seems no one is all that interested in seeing him brought to justice. He's been running his own organized crime syndicate for almost a decade. My guess, he's spread his new wealth around enough to keep him from seeing the first hour behind bars," Bolan stated.

"Well, you're going to love this. Try he's now working with American intelligence."

Bolan managed to hide his surprise.

"Before you get all outraged, understand Drago's been paving the golden road to other crime bosses all the way to Moscow."

"Looking to thin the herd of competition, you mean," the Executioner observed.

"Now we're cynical."

"It's a character flaw. I'm working on it."

Harmon gave a soft snort. "Anyway, what the fat man's doing is helping Uncle Sam track down certain Russian gangsters who are putting the real nasty stuff on the black market for guys who make al-Hamquadra look just a sheep among the wolves."

"So, if this next big move is in the works, why the detour here?"

"Because Drago's offering a cool five mil, U.S., for al-Hamquadra's head."

And there it was again. The money.

"The man has been under CIA tender loving care for some time now," Harmon said. "And unbeknownst to even his own lieutenants, until a few hours ago, he'd already proved a treasure trove against certain Families of the Russian Mafia. Our side cannot afford to lose the intelligence he can provide to shut down the black market proliferation of WMD."

Bolan grunted. "This has to be a first, even for the CIA. A major international crime figure, coddled in the Company's version of a Witness Protection Program."

"That's one way to put it, Mr. Cynical."

"And it doesn't bother anybody he's the gift of crime that keeps on giving drugs, prostitution, extortion, corruption, murder?"

Harmon bobbed his head, seemed to choose his next words carefully. "Okay, I'll grant you, we let him play Don Corleone in exchange, but the vice he peddles is a pale shadow when compared to what some of his competition is out there trying to hawk. You think people are going to stop shooting up and snorting and smoking garbage and whoring and gambling and buying dirty movies and taking bribes to look the other way just because you or anybody else comes along and tells them just because it all looks harmless enough they're still on the road to ruin?" Harmon paused, scouring Bolan a few moments with a hard look, then went on, "A few hours ago I had a nice long chat with the Serb boss to make this deal, a little icing on the cake, if you will, happen."

"Yeah? And how did he feel about his guardian angel just strolling out of the suite to leave him to the fickle fates?" Bolan queried.

"He understands my position, and his role. One, it was a fluke I got grabbed by al-Hamquadra, no more, no less. Two, if he squawked back there, he not only blows my cover, but risks getting his own head lopped off if they find out he's sleeping with American intelligence. Hey, the boss and I aren't exactly going to be drinking buddies, but he's playing ball, and the last thing he wants out in certain circles is he's gone soft. A man of his rep and connections, the intel he can provide the CIA and maybe just hold off World War III, not to mention his favorite mistress and one of his lieutenants getting whacked tonight. You getting the picture here, or do I have to draw it and connect all the dots for you?"

Bolan felt the scowl harden his face. "I'm thinking you're not in the game for all the victims, past, present and future, al-Hamquadra will consume in his legacy before someone checks him out of this world. Nor do you much care if the Serb crime boss gets his pound of flesh."

Harmon chuckled, shook his head. "What it is, Special Agent Cooper, I—we—have a chance to nail the biggest terror threat since bin Laden. In the process of removing this scourge from the face of the Earth, between that twenty mil on al-Hamquadra's head, the five mil Drago is offering for some revenge, and another five mil our side is offering for the capture or disposal of Talliman—yeah, I may love my country, but I know a brass ring when I see one."

"And out of the goodness of your heart you want to cut me in for a piece of the action?"

Harmon played it cool. "Accept the deal. My terms or whatever comes your way at the end of the road here because it sounded like the Serb has some of his own conditions. And I suggest you keep all those bad feelings about Drago to yourself, if you're on board, that is. You say no, I can accept that, too. To show you what a swell guy I am, I'll even get you a ride back to the warm waiting arms of your girlfriend. Sure she's anxious to see you."

"I haven't said no."

"Yet, you mean?"

Bolan shrugged.

"Look, Cooper, if you want in, the offer stands until we get to the end of this road. Drago's my problem, let's be clear on that. If your conscience bothers you about taking what you might think is blood money, then give your slice to some victims' fund or the Justice Department to beef up their resources in the war on terror."

It was an enticing angle, but a thought—and conclusion—the Executioner had already reached.

"So? What's it going to be?"

Bolan hung the moment, staring ahead into the black heart of night, then looked at Harmon and told him, "I'm in."

**19**

"It is but part of my terms. None to be negotiated. In light of your peculiar disappearing act back at the hotel, which, though you explained, I am sure you would agree, were you in my position, Mr. Harmon. I hope your friend is also of like mind."

They were standing in what Harmon knew used to be a study before the Serb gangster converted it into a personal hedonistic heaven. The men had their bags in hand, with five sets of eyes raking them over the coals, all waiting to hear the rest of the gangster's unconditional terms. Worse than whatever the Serb's coming conditions, it didn't look to Harmon the fat SOB would bother to offer them a drink—and this was his safehouse!—when he could sorely use one to wash down the trail dust.

Harmon glanced at his new partner, Cooper's scowl darkening under the revolving light show, the big guy aiming a moment's dark interest toward the trio of Drago's gunslingers on his far right wing. He could tell the Justice Man—if that's what the stone killer even was—was impressed by the obscene digs at Uncle Sam's expense about as much as anything else related to the coming showdown in Algeria.

Not at all.

The money had sealed the deal, that much he reckoned, but strongly suspected the Justice man was working his own agenda into the scheme. Which was part of the reason Harmon wanted him on board to begin with. There was too much he didn't trust about the man, too little he didn't know. In Harmon's world the lethal shadows could come at him from all quarters, deceitful and duplicitous in their own right and up until the bloody end. When this was wrapped in Algeria, he didn't need to be looking over his shoulder for crusaders on any front. And what was to say Cooper hadn't been planted in Barcelona to nail him, and right under his nose at the hotel? Worse, he might have already smelled him out, just waiting for the right moment to eighty-six him and his score. There was a chance, slim at that, he might be able to squeeze the man, once he had him alone, outgunned, staked out in the blazing sun of Algeria, various body parts going under the knife.

Harmon knew he could never be armed with enough knowledge. That alone had more than once hauled his bacon out of the frying pan.

"Is there a problem, Yzet going with you?"

Harmon took a stretched second to act like he was irritated, mulling it over, watching the fat man all scrunched in his big leather throne, stroking his mistress's exposed thigh. "It's your money, but he follows orders and accepts whatever role I define for him."

"Agreed, and it is my five million. A fair price, when I consider some of the most hideous insults I have ever been forced to take, the humiliation I had to bear up under against this Ali-Hamdam creature, the shame I have suffered by the vile tongues of your American media."

"Al-Hamquadra," Harmon said.

"I know his name!" Vikholic suddenly roared, then tossed back the dark liquid in his glass, holding it out for one of the goons to refill, a gunsel quickly stepping forward to fetch another round. "A miserable terrorist dog who is also responsible for the murders of Ilina and one of my best men," the Serb boss snarled. "Yzet, he will go with you to make sure this loathsome insect is crushed. He will make sure, too, he is beheaded, just like he did to the priest. Then you return here with insect's head in a bag where I put it up on mantel. Then you collect your money from me. And only then. Clear?"

Harmon looked at Bolan and said, "You okay with all this?"

"It doesn't sound like we have much of a choice."

"No," Vikholic rasped, "you do not! And I do not care who or what your friend is, Harmon. The terms are the same."

Harmon cut a mean grin. "What the hell, huh, nothing wrong with a few dollars more, since we've come this far."

"What the hell."

Briefly Harmon watched the Justice man take in the surroundings, then square the competition, saw the same penetrating scour of the soul for the Serbs that he'd gone under the guy's microscope back at the hotel, measuring, picking apart, wheels spinning. It left him wondering what was really going on behind those ice blue eyes, though he had his suspicions. On the way into the safehouse it hadn't escaped his notice that Cooper had been absorbing the lay of the building and perimeter, taking into account the two sentries—Harmon's own guys—armed and posted out front, looking for weak points, the easiest breaching zones, he guessed.

Harmon addressed Vikholic as he snatched his drink from the hired gun. "We have a few hours to kill before we're in the air. I'll need to brief your man, in private. Any chance I can at least take a look at your money before we leave?"

"It will be here before noon. It will remain here with me until you return."

Harmon spun on his heel. "If that's all…"

"Not quite."

Harmon spied that strange fire burning brighter, deeper in the Justice man's eyes. It was a look Harmon had come to know and read well in their short time together.

"You will succeed, yes? You will not fail, correct?"

Before Harmon could answer, the Justice man told Vikholic, "You can count on it."

And that voice, Harmon decided, rivaled the granite expression, like nothing he'd ever heard, or seen.

Cold and unforgiving as Death itself.

**20**

Akhmedah al-Hamquadra peered toward the long spool of
dust trailing the white Mercedes stretch limousine. Shifting on
his haunches in the rocky crevice perched above the Wadi
Ghoulat, he lifted high-powered field glasses. A sweep of the
cobalt heavens above revealed no aircraft. He panned the barren wasteland at the northern edges of the Grand Erg Orien-
tal stretched before him. Nothing, he found, but parched
lunarlike desolation to the east and north, with smooth undu-
lating waves of brown sand to the south, the panorama baking
under the watching eye of the midafternoon sun. He surveyed
distant heat mirages finally, grimly aware nothing was really
as it seemed in such an empty ocean of rock, dirt and sand.

In truth, the seeming absence of life was often the enemy's
best friend, a cloak the capable warrior knew how to wear to
his advantage while stalking. He could ill afford to leave anything to chance, not after Barcelona.

While al-Hamquadra waited on the man coming to him
from Touggourt, where he kept one of dozens of rumored
safehouses scattered across North Africa, he gave the edge of
the rise a quick search, found his shooters still in place,
stretched out on their stomachs, as still as pieces of stone. His
snipers, four in all, wielding Russian Dragunovs with RPGs

at their fingertips, were nearly invisible to the naked eye. Like him, they donned buff-colored clothing, from boots to kaffiyeh, and kept low to the hard-packed earth, using scrub for cover wherever possible. In this stretch of burning nothingness, with only a few villages scattered between here and the border with Tunisia, it would be easy enough for the enemy to mark their hiding place with their satellites or recon birds. That was assuming the infidels knew where to look.

Which led him to the dilemma of the immediate future.

As agreed upon, he was to pay the American intelligence handlers a hefty fee of twelve million dollars U.S. for their role in the hotel operation. That, he knew, was eight million shy of the blood money placed on his own head. Thus the bottom line, from where they stood.

Money.

Yes, they had served their purpose, and admirably so, the State Department man lured into his grasp and now being sat on in the abandoned village of Joubal Sourel two kilometers north. What, though, was to say their treachery would not follow him to Algeria? What was to say they hadn't fielded a small covert force to land here and hunt him down? Twenty million dollars was no small fortune, and he personally knew of Iraqi policemen who had killed, provided him intelligence and safe passage for a pitiful twenty dollars U.S, if only to feed their starving families one more day. These shadow men were, after all, still the enemy, only now they served their own greed, money the only god they bowed to. They had no ideals, no vision, no principles. And if they had no qualms about murdering their own people, then how could he think himself exempt from their savagery once they received final payment? Weren't they, too, like the very devils he was at war against, born and bred of Western greed and malice that knew no bounds? Indoctrinated by their government, military and media to view those beyond the seething wickedness of their culture as subhumans?

That in mind, the shadow men were loose ends, and he determined there was only one way to tie it all up. Before that time came upon them, where he knotted the bloody bow, he first needed to know what else they knew, and beyond the State Department jackal. Trusting them—even though they had come to him via cutouts, and perhaps could have killed him several times before he met with one of them in Cairo—was never an option. Naturally, many of his freedom fighters—most of whom were now dead, he was sure, back in Barcelona—would have never agreed to accept on what appeared blind faith inside help from infidels. Now he was down to a mere ten warriors in his immediate circle who had been deigned worthy enough to leave Barcelona by boat.

The good news, here in Algeria, was that his exploits were admired by the Armed Islamic Group, the GIA. More impressed than ever, flush with success in Barcelona, Bhetal Khourab, leader of the Phalanx of Death splinter group, had personally assured that al Hamquadra and his fighters would be would safe in his country. He was honored to be chosen for such noble service in jihad. Of course, a large cache of weapons and a steamer trunk of euros had solidified the GIA's vow of protection, the Algerian freedom fighter beefing up his own depleted force with an additional thirty-four holy warriors.

When the limousine braked near an outcrop shaped in a semicircle as agreed upon, al-Hamquadra gathered up his AK-74 and proceeded down the incline.

The man was known to him only as the Financier. He had never met the man, nor seen a photo of him. All communication, up to this point, was done through a series of couriers trusted to martyr themselves should they be cornered by the enemy. Rumor was the Financier was connected to the Saudi royal family, a distant cousin of a distant cousin, but those who were even remotely close to the oil spigots in that country, al-Hamquadra knew, were rich beyond the wildest fantasies of any Arab warrior, nomad, or peasant faithful to the strict tenets of Islam.

Money, he had to confess, would always wield true power in any culture, any faith. That, and the sword, of course.

Al-Hamquadra was on level ground, a sheet of dust drifting past him, when the blacked-out window on the driver's side slid down by electronic touch. Assault rifle kept low by his leg but ready to sweep up and blast at the first sign of trouble, the terrorist leader took a gust of ice-cold air in the face as he braked near the door. He could be sure the vehicle was armor-plated, bulletproof glass and such, tires reinforced by Kevlar bands even, but that wouldn't stop him from rolling both grenades under the chassis if...

"He is anxious to meet with the American. What about the others?"

Al-Hamquadra peered over the head of the bearded driver to the black partition that sealed off the well. "They are due to arrive shortly." He took his handheld radio and ordered Abu to bring the jeep down with the others. "You will follow us."

"Are you not going to ask about the money?"

"Why? I assume you brought it. Unless there was a problem?"

"We have it. No problem. We will follow."

Al-Hamquadra walked away, satisfied all was going according to plan as he saw the Russian-made jeep pull out of the hidden depression halfway up the slope. He was anxious to conclude his business with the American intelligence operatives. What they didn't know was a lot.

In fact, their ignorance and greed was about to get them killed.

He had other plans on how to spend their money.

THE SPECTER OF DIRE STRAITS began to rise as Bolan hit the ground at the end of the six-hundred-foot combat jump from the black ferrite-painted transport plane. The chute wadded up and now buried with his pack as quickly as he could, beneath a litter of strewed rocks, the Executioner took up the M-16 M-203 assault rifle combo and fell back into a narrow fissure slashed into the earth.

Scanning the broken moonscape through night-vision goggles, Bolan hoped he was all but invisible in the thick cloak of blackness. It was but one of several grim factors in the forefront of the soldier's mind that Harmon and his men were likewise outfitted with high-tech eyes to peer into the night.

He performed another long search of the landscape, waiting for Harmon to patch through over the com link. A watch check revealed the call was nearly two minutes late. Another thirty seconds, still nothing. He considered keying the headset, but nagging gut instinct warned him his troubles had only just begun, and went way beyond any kind of radio silence.

He was being set up, the wrong edge of the blade all but poised to tear out his throat.

There was little doubt al-Hamquadra was on the scene, once he saw it all through Harmon's perspective—greed—but the soldier would paint bull's-eyes on anyone armed and angry from that point on. Damn, but he had his suspicions Harmon was dirty back in Barcelona, and now, he was sure, they were edging closer to panning out to bitter dark truth, with his number up, his hide to be held over the abyss. But what the hell was he exactly to Harmon? A bargaining chip? A scapegoat of some type? Why? For what?

How to proceed?

Simple.

Stalk and kill. End of game. Same deal if they lied under whatever questioning he could grab on the run.

The soldier followed the black transport plane as it banked toward him, straightening next from its sudden aborted west vector. That course would have the transport about a half mile or more farther out than his own jump. It was now aimed for Tunisia, and, according to Harmon's scheme, the pilot was supposed to return in a few short hours for exfiltration at a pre-arranged LZ farther east, allegedly on the ground and waiting.

Later, if ever, on that front.

First problems tackled first.

Whatever the customized wonders of high-tech, though, engine noise sounded muffled to his ears, as the C-47 look-alike began to vanish. Harmon's ride had all the ultra-trimmings for covert ops, which told Bolan the guy had major backing somewhere up the chain of command. The one scintilla of good news was the sum total of gadgetry at Harmon's command had gotten them the seven hundred miles and change from Barcelona to the east edge of the world's worst country.

So far undetected, unscathed.

And out in the middle of nowhere.

Stranded.

On his own, and up against what? How many savages, in reality, beyond what Harmon had told him?

Bolan hauled in his war bag, unzipped it for ready access. He slipped the Uzi across a shoulder, watching the green ghostland framed in night vision, then threaded a sound suppressor to his Beretta 93-R. Harmon was, supposedly, right behind him, out the door. In a drop that short, drift wasn't a factor. Harmon was on the ground, Bolan could bet on it. Where? Smart money told him the agent was either hiding—in ambush?—or making fast tracks to the terror camp.

Or had left behind one of the Killer Bees—as the four operatives on the ground were tagged—to carry out whatever Harmon's wet work or treacherous agenda for him.

Quickly, scouting for any sign of movement in the rocky slopes to the north and west, the Executioner ran down what he knew. Enemy numbers of Joubal Sourel were roughly fifty, give or take, the direction of the terror stronghold three klicks northwest, the Wadi Ghoulat able to plant him close to the enemy's back door. Recalling Harmon's show and tell during the flight, the village was once a haven for extremists, but bore clear evidence of MiG strikes by the Algerian military to vaporize GIA savages with napalm pounding. The Killer Bees were supposed to have made the camp's outer perimeter by now, recon, report to Harmon, but hold up. The plan was for one of the operatives to move in and mine the motor pool with plastic explosive once they were all linked up, the rest of Harmon's hitters setting out to form a ring of fire around the small village. They'd wade in when the fireworks started, pick off all comers, seal it up on the march in. It was hardly the best laid strategy, when Bolan considered al-Hamquadra was marked down to be a confirmed kill…

Wait a second!

Twenty million dollars, the Executioner recalled. That was the asking price for the cannibal's head, first come, first served, but were there other top-tier butchers lined up here in Harmon's gunsights with six or seven figures for their carcasses? A few million more, what the hell, as long as Harmon was in the neighborhood. The puzzle had sordid and bloody pieces all over the map, but he was seeing them now wanting to fit, one at time. What he suspected was that al-Hamquadra had been running the show in both the killing suite and hotel, then had simply walked out right before the raid was launched, for one. It didn't make sense that the world's most wanted terrorist had overlooked Harmon, the operative's hands free the whole time, weapon in his coat pocket. Piece two. Harmon holding back during their two-man run and gun, as if he had something too valuable to risk losing in any attempt to save innocent lives, what now struck Bolan as a token effort, more show than go. Twenty million bucks had seemed to drop out of nowhere and onto Harmon's radar screen no sooner had he cleared the hotel, as if al-Hamquadra was practically begging him to come and collect. Harmon the mystery man who had all the right answers for all the wrong moves. Dump a Serb crime boss and his five mil, a State Department traitor with what equaled divine knowledge of terror operations into the caldron, stir up the whole fetid brew...

Funny how the truth rarely set a man in his position free, Bolan thought. If Harmon was in league with the devil during the hotel seige but now intended to stab the Executioner in the back and score a fat payday...

There was no point in cursing the hand he'd been dealt and freely accepted. The truth was, Bolan experienced a moment of morbid relief it had come down to him against them, that he was believed by them to be their fish out of water to be gutted for reasons yet to be determined. He could be wrong, but he'd be shocked to the marrow of his bones if it turned out any other way.

Bolan slipped the war bag over his free shoulder. He didn't like the added weight, aware speed was the better part of the game plan now, as he checked the lay of the land with one last sweep. But the only way, he knew, to lighten the load was to start using it up. He broke from cover, hauling himself for what was the shortest stretch across a no-man's land toward the broken chain of low hills to the north.

Beyond there waited Joubal Sourel.

And where the Executioner knew he'd find the human storm, gathered and waiting to blow. Whether or not he discovered some sordid truth in the coming hour or so he already had his own role defined. Cannibal or traitor, it didn't matter.

The menu was full, priced high, but they were all fair and bloody game for an Executioner special.

**21**

James Talliman thought he was going to vomit when he saw what was on the laptop's monitor. The terror was bad enough, but he found it strange, somewhat comforting, truth be told, how he had come to accept the adrenaline surges, the thunder of runaway heartbeats in his ears, since he was dumped on the cabin cruiser a few blocks beyond the hotel, where his hands were bound with rope, a hood dropped over his head. As the hours dragged into one eternity after another—manhandled onto what he knew was a helicopter before landing God only knew where and being hauled to his final destination by vehicle—the iron grip of clawing fear and blackening depression telling him he was so far removed from the first speck of civilization, meaning the Western World, had nearly plunged him to despair.

Now...

He almost wished they'd left him blind, as he looked away from the group of hooded or headclothed armed killers in the far corner of the large stone hovel. Judging from the modems attached to the notebook computer and the manner in which the fingers of one of the killers flew over keyboard, the image and whatever the rabble-rousing diatribe attached being hurtled through cyberspace. No doubt CD-ROMs would be burned for future dispersal, to be used as either recruitment tools or to bolster any weak and faltering faith in the group's Muslim brethren. How many Internet chat rooms would view the grisly horror of the priest being decapitated? he wondered. How long before al-Jazeera ran the sick ghoul show for Muslim fanatics he was sure would clap and shout in twisted glee?

Screw all that! How was he going to get out of there with his own head still on his shoulders?

Hours ago, the fanatics had dumped him in his own corner of hell, the wooden chair groaning under his weight suddenly as his body stiffened in reaction to the repulsive sight of such a cold-blooded and gruesome execution. And, he thought, murder of a man of God, no less. Why, though, did he expect a priest to be hands-off, sacred to animals who wantonly and by the countless scores slaughtered anybody else? One thing for sure, if he had ever doubted the existence of evil, that Satan was alive and well and roamed the earth in search of fertile ground in the dark hearts of men, then all he had to do was sit there, watch, and quake, terrified, in its presence. And yet...

Had he not been willing to sell them intelligence, trading his own soul, in fact, and for money? As a man who knew the enemies of the free world clamored to spread their evil, a man who did, in truth, gather classified intelligence to fight the menace of terrorism...

And what was with this sudden waver of conscience? Was it simply fear of being murdered? Or was it that he knew what he had up to then schemed would demand an accounting? That there was, in fact, some horror and agony incomprehensible to man's finite puny powers of reason and knowledge waiting for him on the other side? And what kind of sniveling coward was he becoming now anyway? Thinking of God, demanding God show up and real quick and save him from possible torture, or murder and perdition? Did God answer prayers in the trench, when all looked lost and everything schemed and chased by some miserable wretch was being dashed to ruin and despair? He hadn't seen the inside of a church since he married his now estranged wife. Now his mind was fairly screaming in madness, and for some invisible power to descend through the roof and slay everything in sight in some supernatural sudden calamity that would set him free, unscathed and fleeing into the night!

Which was more fantastic and sordid in its lunacy? That he could still sell out his own country and hope to save himself by the very act of treason while becoming a rich man? Or that divine justice would magically appear because he was terrified of dying and he demanded it now to bail him out of the fire, immolate these animals in the process while granting him mercy? What about his money? What about all the people sure to eventually discover—if they hadn't already—what he'd done? They'd seek the kind of vengeance that demanded blood justice.

Sucking in long deep breaths, certain he was on the verge of losing any and all grip on tenuous sanity, he went back to watching the lunatic who was hard at work downloading some of his files, his laptop set on a table just a few feet to his side, like the bastard wanted only to taunt him some more in his utter helplessness.

That was the answer, he decided. Why didn't he think of it before? Why worry? Until he was positive he would be set free, however, with money in his numbered Swiss account, he determined to hold on to three last access codes that would break open the gates to the rest of the mother lode.

Okay, calm down, he told himself. Keep the trump card close to the vest, surely the first and last key to salvation. Dangle a piece of gold, here and there, but give a little, get a little.

He was about to distract himself with more regret over how this all could have possibly happened when the wool blanket on the other side of the room was swept aside and a short, slight figure with assault rifle marched in.

Talliman felt his heart sink into his stomach. Now, unmasked and looking him in the eye…

"Mr. Talliman," Akhmedah al-Hamquadra said, smiling. "I hope you have had enough rest from the long trip."

"Where the hell have you taken me?"

"Never mind that. Our time ahead may be shortened by circumstances beyond my control, so I will urge you to consider strongly that whatever comes out of your mouth next will be the truth about ongoing operations your country has launched against myself and my fellow brothers around the world."

Talliman suspected the world's most wanted terrorist already knew he had much more to offer than what was on his laptop hard drive. He did. Thus he weighed his next words, wondering how to work in the monetary reward angle, while getting a commitment to his personal safety in the same breath. He caught a moment's reprieve next, as the world's number-one scourge fell into group banter with the other militants, all voices low and speaking back and forth in Arabic. Then, he watched, as three more swarthy types rolled through the curtain. Two of them, dressed in sport shirts and brown khakis, AK-47s slung around their shoulders, dumped four large nylon bags in the middle of the dirt floor. He could almost smell all that money, figured ten million or more if those were hundreds bulging the sacks. Before they noticed his lingering gaze for what it was, he noted number three was dressed in an expensive silk suit jacket and matching slacks, smelled an arrogant bearing about the man. The guy might as well have hung a sign over his head that he was some kind of hotshot fundamentalist power broker. Tall and wiry, his beard flowing out from a kaffiyeh that partially hid his face, the man took a post off to the side of al-Hamquadra, eyes observing everything from behind black sunglasses.

More conversation.

Talliman, shirt plastered to clammy flesh already baked during the day's stifling heat, felt fresh beads of sweat pop out on his forehead, the air growing thicker with the force of their dark menacing presence. He was all but ready to give up the whole store, if only to save his miserable hide, watching as al-Hamquadra turned his way, the smile gone to stone. Was the assault rifle swinging a few inches his direction? Was…

He felt his lips parting, the cry rising in his throat when the door crashed open. Talliman was ready to dump himself to the floor, the atmosphere crackling with fear. The moment hung for what seemed an hour, as he was braced for shooting that never came. Somehow he managed to turn his head, all those gun muzzles in full view, just the same, and found a white-haired gate-crasher with an Uzi shoving a militant he used as a shield into the room.

"Everybody just relax. If I wanted you dead, you'd already be on your way to Hell."

"Mr. Harmon," al-Hamquadra said, as cool as a fall breeze, the smile back and frozen in place. "Please, join us. I have been expecting you."

THE EXECUTIONER TOOK the sting out of the first Killer Bee with the Beretta 93-R. Bridging the distance to the dark shadow in three long strides, Bolan hit the top end of the slender gully hard, the black op grunting and cursing as he flopped down, hand grabbing at the bloody ragged edges where the 9 mm subsonic rounds had shattered his collarbone. The hardman threw out the arm just as Bolan lashed out with a kick and sent the HK-33 assault rifle spinning away, smacking into a slab of rock partition. A swift kick to the guts drove the wind out of the sentry on a guttural belch, immobilizing him long enough for the Stony Man warrior to flip him over on his stomach, fasten hands behind his back with plastic cuffs, rip off the night-vision headgear. Sticking the sound-suppressed muzzle in the man's ear turned the guy to stone.

Bolan stole a few moments to review, assess, get his bearings. It was quiet along the ridge, an utter stillness in the chilly air, beyond and below. If they were there, they would come any second.

Breathe, scan, probe.

The soldier looked at his prisoner. He had spotted him only moments before he'd hit the low hill's back end, the gully revealing itself out of nowhere at the last second before he plunged on. It was a fluke, catching the buzz-cut head on the fly, a desperate gamble next, gathering instant speed, risking it all in hopes there was only one armed combatant in the vicinity. One Killer Bee down, and the Executioner again peered into the darkness all around him, combat senses torqued and probing for the slightest hint of movement. Nothing.

"What the hell, I thought we were on the same team?"

Bolan paused again, briefly recalling how the man used his handle, "Crusader," then the feral look he'd spotted a split second before the HK-33 began to swing his way. Clearly, the guy had thought he could just waltz him straight into a bullet, but he'd only fooled himself. Bolan had seen enough of

Harmon already to know he was now staring down at the same piece of nasty work. Sure, it would have been easier to eliminate a menace on the way in, cover his six, but Bolan needed information, and assuming the long-term came beyond the next hour, a prisoner of this ilk could prove invaluable.

The Executioner borrowed some more ticks on the doomsday clock, scouting the terrain to the north. It was broken tableland, but the wadi still looked his best and quickest shot, arrow straight, in fact, right to the enemy's camp. There was just enough sheen from whatever the source of light on the other side of the distant ridge—generator-powered lights or fire barrels—to guide the soldier's intended hard charge.

Bolan dragged his prisoner down into the gully until he felt he was no longer an easy sitting target. "Your name?"

"Banner."

"I ask the questions. I won't repeat myself. If I feel you're lying, I'll kill you. Come clean, and there's a chance you walk out of here."

"I come clean, Harmon will kill me."

"Which of us is your biggest problem in the here and now?"

Banner's look was torn between a scowl and a grimace of pain. "I'm listening."

"How do I fit into Harmon's plans?"

"He needs you to deflect some of the heat."

Bolan checked the gully, then put pressure on the Beretta. "Riddles will get you killed as quick as lies. Two seconds, Banner. One…"

"Harmon volunteers me to hang back for the ambush job! We take some Kodak moments of your corpse, get your fingerprints, dress up a few extremists to make it look like you went berserk on some unarmed nomads, haul your body with us, if possible. We work certain sources back in the States, dump what we have on you at the *Washington Post, New York Times,* a few of the more liberal talking heads, like that. Major scandal. Intelligence community, the White House, Pentagon scrambling for cover. The flak this administration's been taking—Abu Ghraib, the whole war in Iraq, any number of rumors, for that matter—there's a lot of people willing to believe and promote the worst. Conspiracy nuts, lunatic fringe, the PC crowd, they all need their big scapegoat. And after the operation in Barcelona, whoever you really are and whoever you work for—and Harmon would find out eventually, believe me—you and your people become the sacrificial goats."

"Take the blame for the operation Harmon or his cutouts hatched with al-Hamquadra. Cover your asses."

"In a nutshell. We were going to use the State guy…"

"But I just happened along."

"Like manna from heaven. Harmon had you pegged as one of us first time he laid eyes on you, so he says."

"He's wrong on both counts."

"Yeah, right. Looks more like you're some nightmare come boiling straight out of Hell. And for what it's worth, I thought Harmon was crazy to bring you in to begin with."

"You ever hear of free will?"

"Now who's talking in riddles?"

"You could have told Harmon to stick it."

"It's about more than just money, friend."

Bolan gave his surroundings another sweep. "Keep talking."

"There are certain people on our side who don't want this war on terror to end. No truce, no declaration of even the first hint of a remote victory."

"A few back home think they're above the rules give the

marching orders, you mean. Sit back and profit off everybody else's blood and misery," Bolan stated.

"That's the general idea. The way this select group on our side sees it, they want the shadow war against terror to go on forever, or until their own game is in place."

"Which is?"

"Dominion over all the earth. I may be stating the obvious to a guy like you, the names and the faces change all the time with each high value target we take out, but there will always be another al-Hamquadra to step up and keep it going. Shit, these people back in the States, they ship guys like me and Harmon out here to create, train and arm a lot of this rabid-ass rabble. You know why? So they can keep their own comfort and security and good times rolling and their personal fortunes growing to obscene excess while at the same time keep feeding the fuel to their own vision of a New World Order," the operative explained.

"Grab their slice of the pie while it's fat?"

"It goes way beyond Iraq and a few small arms deals or some million tons of explosive ordnance the world at large may hear about. Yesterday's good friend is tomorrow's worst enemy, but that's the way the shadows on our side want to keep it. A guessing game as to who the good guys really are. Shadows inside shadows, riddles inside riddles, that's how they keep fomenting each new crisis."

"Throw gasoline on the fire," Bolan suggested.

"The world's getting too small too quick for them. They know Armageddon will happen someday soon enough, it's just a question to them of how big a holocaust and how to contain it."

"So, why not get it over with since it's bound to happen. And out of the ashes they arise."

"Just like the Phoenix."

"Every man, woman and child on the planet not strong enough or doesn't have money enough to fend for themselves falls by the wayside," Bolan said.

"That's how they've got it on the drawing board. If John and Jane Q. Public knew some things we know, is the UN holding hands with Saddam in their food for oil scam would look clean as a newborn's ass in comparison," the operative told him.

"The table being set for the Apocalypse."

"Think about it. The average citizen is just a number in cyberspace nowadays. The information highway is a major part of their power base which the masses just blindly hand over to them without the first damn thought. The dawn of the computer age, it all looks harmless enough, Internet, e-mail, but cyberspace, that's their way of expanding the evolution of civilization as they see it. To your average Joe Geek, all this computer technology, the expansion of global telecommunication in all its forms is all for the benefit and betterment of mankind, creating jobs and services and like that, when, in truth, we are being marked and stamped and tracked by, yeah, I'll say it, the sign of the Beast.

"These people, they want power, total control in a world they feel is fast slipping beyond their present reach of power and control. The Apocalypse is not a question of can or will it happen, but when. I'm telling you, there are people you'd never suspect hard at it right now who want it to happen sooner rather than later, and with them calling the shots."

"Save themselves. Make their fortunes. Whoever they deem fit to live can serve them in their new world. That about the size of it?" Bolan asked.

"The end game. Save the planet, expand their dominion.

Thin the world's human herd to a manageable point. You want the short list? Right now the people backing up Harmon are ready to run covert tactical nuclear strikes, or initiate 'bio-cleansing,' they call it. Syria. Iran. North Korea, even parts of Russia. Believe it. It's in the works. They've got Iraqi oil already grasped in their iron fist. The Saudis are next up, I hear. Then Sudan, Angola, those hellholes are capable of pumping out more black gold by the day on their own than our 'friends,' the Saudis. Don't want to play ball, you say? Think about it while your people eat some Level Four virus or get fried to a shadow on the sidewalk by a mushroom cloud."

Banner went quiet, deathly still, as if he was exhausted, or suddenly terrified he had said far too much.

The Executioner had come up against this New World Order mantra before, and he believed what Banner told him was, more or less, on the money. Some of those entrusted with the power to uphold law and order were working behind the scenes to save their futures and swell to obscene proportions their personal wealth at the expense and horror of myriads of innocents. They reasoned the ills of the human race were due to the simple fact there were too many mouths to feed, prime real estate—their own jealously guarded enclaves of paradise on Earth—being swarmed and trampled by subhuman invasion. Along the dark lines of this twisted thinking, terror and greed blurred all reason over the dreaded reality of inevitable dwindling resources, Earth's burgeoning population threatening to unleash disease, famine, the daily growing legions of desperate poor and borderline starving masses consuming ever-shrinking wealth the shadow powers had to grab up before it was all gone.

Peace on Earth? Forget about it.

Whether it was Alexander's army with shield and spear or the shadow players of the New World Order wielding technology that Man believed would put him one step closer to being God it boiled down to the same damn thing.

Death and destruction. Power and dominion for a self-anointed few at a hellish plight of untold misery and suffering for the many.

Under any nation's banner, by any argument hurled about to convince themselves they were right, it was all still what it was.

Evil.

There were too many questions hung in limbo, too many faces hidden in the dark beyond Algeria Bolan may or may never hunt down, but he had more than enough to take it from there in the immediate grim present. Unless he missed his guess all roads were then leading toward the cannibals turning on one another.

And that, also, would work to his advantage.

He didn't have a second more to waste. Banner would keep when he coldcocked and gagged him.

The Executioner applied pressure to the Beretta. "All this revelation according to Banner, but I get the feeling you're holding back."

"The hell you say."

"I want details about Harmon's real play on his twenty-million-dollar trophy and quick. Or hell you will know."

IF HARMON HADN'T SEEN it with his own eyes he wouldn't have believed it. There was fear and indecision for at least four or five seconds in the eyes of the planet's current number-one human plague.

Perfect.

Now was the moment to nail it down.

Give it up. Money or their lives.

Harmon held out the GIA shield, a fist wadding up the shoulder of the man's robe, Uzi aimed rock-steady on al-Hamquadra. "I don't know whether to laugh or shoot. By the way, those three sentries you posted understand now they're serious when they say cigarette smoking kills."

"I think I know you."

"Shut your hole," Harmon growled at Talliman, edging his human shield a step closer toward the militants. Eight serpents in the nest, he counted, listening hard for any noise beyond the blanket hung over the doorway on the other side. "Braxton!" he snarled over his shoulder, heard his man respond to the call, slipping into the doorway to back his play.

"Right here, sir."

"How we looking out there, soldier?" Harmon asked.

"Baldwin still has our six, sir. Thirty meters out back and holding. Benson's perch east and south, sir, motor pool covered. All packages armed and ready. You give the word, Benson lights it up."

"Hear that?" Harmon told al-Hamquadra. "If anybody here gets a fanatical wild hair not only does my man take out your rides away from here and bring down a wall or two in the process, he dumps a few RPGs on your heads to nail the coffins shut."

"And to what end?" al-Hamquadra said, holding up a hand, waving down his men. "You die, no money."

"That's right. If I don't get what I want nobody does. Heaven or Hell, nothing in between for me and my guys. And if I really wanted to kill you—all of you—I could have simply called in an air strike, maybe lobbed down a Tomahawk or two on this whole dung pile."

"If it's the money you want, there it is. Twelve million for the delivery of Mr. Talliman, as agreed with your man in Egypt."

"I'll get to that, and try real hard now to remember what you said about patience to Colonel Alvarado back in Barcelona. FYI, Akhmadah, what's in those bags isn't near enough to tide me over for the never-ending party I have in my mind, once I jump my own people's sinking ship."

Al-Hamquadra scowled. "You want the twenty million dollars your country has put on my head."

"It's all negotiable, and it's not how it might sound. We can work it out where you keep breathing to keep on spreading your sunshine. But we need to leave and get you and me to where I can freely and without fear for my life work out the details."

"And Talliman?"

"Your people can have him. Skin him alive and film it for all I care. Whatever he has I have it all in the world's best computer—my own brain."

"What the hell are you telling them?" Talliman squawked. "Do you have any idea who I—"

"Braxton!"

Harmon sensed Talliman knew what was coming, as the man stopped whining and he felt Braxton sweeping past. "Don't move!" he warned the militants, al-Hamquadra cursing in Arabic, but all their weapons locked to frozen.

Braxton drew a bead with his HK-33 on Talliman who screamed, "No! Don't! For the love of—"

The short blister of autofire ringing in his ears, Harmon roared, "I have his access codes! Move a muscle and I start shooting!"

Al-Hamquadra was livid, spittle flying from his lips as he snarled, "How do you have them?"

"I had a man crack his hard drive while he was sipping his fourth gin martini in the restaurant before it hit the fan." Harmon heard the shouts from somewhere down the ruins. "Get one of your men outside now and calm the troops or I start blasting and I start with you! How I get that twenty million on your head doesn't matter to me."

As one of the militants stepped forward at the terrorist leader's urging, Harmon ordered Braxton, "Get those bags in some wheels that aren't primed, but grab a couple of our friends here to walk them there."

**22**

The kaffiyeh didn't fool Bolan. One 9 mm parabellum round from the leading Beretta, and Killer Bee Two had his lights punched out for good. Assuming Banner told the truth, that would leave Killer Bees Braxton and Baldwin latched to Harmon's hip.

At this point, the soldier knew it didn't matter. He was there to finish it.

As he shadowed down the gully, sidearm and M-16 scanning the ridge and slope, he sidestepped the corpse of the extremist sentry with the back of his skull blown apart and fell in beside the late sniper Banner called Benson. The question as to why it had seemed too damn easy to climb his way out of the wadi and into the present launch position at the southeast edge of the camp became readily apparent to the Executioner.

Up close, the village showed grim evidence of air strikes, with blackened twisted skeletons of vehicles littered around the edges of rubble that once stood as decent-sized stone dwellings. A smattering of tents formed a half-ring to the west, the picture pretty much laid out as Harmon detailed. Armed shadows in hoods and kaffiyehs were now rolling in a large wave from the tents and fire barrels, with one single destination in collective mind. Bolan saw that one hut, larger than the ruins, still stood, oddly untouched by the recent bombardment save for a couple of jagged holes in the south facade.

Inside that hut Bolan heard the commotion that was commanding enemy attention all over the camp. Silhouettes, maybe three in all, flickered about in light spilling inside from the kerosene lamp hung on the back door. Voices were locked in angry back and forth dialogue, the loudest of which the soldier pegged as belonging to Harmon.

Just about show time.

The Executioner spotted the det box beside Benson's HK-33 assault rifle with fixed scope, RPG-7 and a bag opened to reveal a half-dozen or so warheads. The red light was on, the doomsday package good to go. How much of the motor pool was juiced to blow remained to be seen. At least twenty vehicles were strung out in a ragged line, starting at the east side of the camp. Other than the curious sight of a white stretch limo, the rides were standard terror wheels: battered SUVs, two vans, a few Algerian versions of the dreaded Technicals, those vehicles more infamous in such countries as Sudan and Somalia where machine guns and rocket pods were mounted in the beds. One of those Technicals was pulling away from the motor pool, braking near the north edge of the main hut. The distance was roughly sixty, seventy meters tops, but Bolan made out the buzz cut manning the wheel. Braxton or Baldwin, no matter. A quick but harder look, and the soldier spied the bulk of a nylon bag jutting over the edge of the Technical's bed. He could assume, then, that was some of Harmon's loot in the getaway wheels.

It seemed to the soldier that the bad guys were at each other's throats, demo work already done for him. Some fat cash was ready to be swiped and dumped into that special victims fund Harmon had mentioned, and he hadn't broken a sweat so far. Bolan figured he had to be living right.

Sensing he was clear and all the ravenous wolves were gathering, the Executioner hauled out a LAW rocket launcher. He settled for the RPG-7, sighted down on the band of militants, gauging the distance.

Rock and roll.

A second after he triggered the warhead, whooshing on its way, Bolan depressed the single button on the det box.

Massive peals of thunder and blinding light erupted, broken bodies and wreckage hurtled in all directions. Fireballs boiled toward the sky, but the blasts merely lit the fuse for the Executioner to nail down doomsday.

WHATEVER THE STORM AND its source, Harmon knew that was no ticker tape parade and marching band come to celebrate his victory. He had his suspicions about the identity of the attacker, but now was not the moment to condemn himself for arrogance and ambition. If, in fact, it was Cooper...

What he knew for certain was that one second he was on the move to grab al-Hamquadra by the scruff of his neck, the next thing he saw in his angry scope was half the east wall coming down. Winging bats of demolished vehicles came pounding behind the meteors of stone hurtled through the room, the shower bowling down the opposition, with shock waves and rubble knocking him off his feet like a giant fist. There were stars in his eyes, bile in his throat, jackhammers in his ears...

No time to dawdle over a little pain and discomfort.

Harmon knew he had but a split second to pull it together, as he heard the terrorists hacking, found them staggering to rise in the swirling tempest of smoke and dust. He hauled himself to his feet, blood in his mouth and stinging into his eyes, but the Uzi was up and flaming. Harmon viciously cursed the moment and this sudden unexplained calamity, terrified the series of explosions had ripped through the money bags.

Focus!

He took it all out on the extremist rabble, the sight of them getting stitched and chewed to standing, spinning ribbons nearly bringing on a jolt of joy. Sliding away from the door, as they returned fire, Harmon screamed obscenities at the top of his lungs. He heard yet two, maybe three more explosions erupt somewhere in the motor pool.

Son of a bitch!

Harmon kept drilling the militants, left to right, a few more rounds, here and there for good sadistic measure, as he bellowed curses into the hellish tumult of his Uzi volley and the sonic booms beyond. In the corner of his eye, he spied Braxton bull into the seething caldron of blood and shredded cloth, the man's HK-33 hurling more furious clamor into the din. Firing on, sweeping the Uzi back in sync with Braxton's firing line hose job, Harmon watched, as enemy gunners flailed into twitching whirlwinds, AKs blazing still. Harmon felt rounds scorching past his ears, too close for comfort and threatening to snatch away the big score.

Over there! The rotten cowards!

Three fanatics, he saw, were at the end of their lightning-bolt surge, plowing through the curtain, one of them triggering his AK-74, but missing high and wide. They were partly obscured by all the smoke and flotsam veiling the air, but Harmon was fairly positive he knew who two of them were, racing like they were on fire to flee this abattoir.

Feeding another 32-round magazine to his Uzi, Harmon led Braxton to the door. There, he was greeted by more explosions, as he went low by the door, looking left. Baldwin was still doing a righteous number, militants dropping, bloody human dominoes to the west, the air ripped asunder by sharp grunts and howls of pain between rattling bursts of autofire and yet two more thundering blasts. Seven or eight jihadists were spraying weapons fire in several directions.

Harmon hit the Israeli subgun's trigger as warped hulks of trash slammed to earth, sliced off the roof above. "Go!"

Braxton didn't have to be told twice, the man tearing past Harmon, on the fly for the Technical holding the money. It sure as hell didn't look the best laid plan under the circumstances, but Harmon knew, coming in, there was no other play than to out-Murphy Murphy.

Which meant only the biggest Godzilla pair with the highest raised middle finger on this block would skip on out of this kind of slaughter and insanity.

Something suddenly felt even more calamitous and on the way than the hovel's wall blowing up in his face. Skulls were being blasted apart downrange, two, then three more fanatics toppling hard, but the direction in which they were hammered down...

Backpedaling, about to throw himself into a one-eighty, Harmon snatched an eyefull of Baldwin's corpse, sprawled in an ungainly crucifixion up the slope. Screams and shouts were flaying the air worse than ever, it seemed, another unholy peal of thunder shattering his senses. He howled as he felt the fire lance into his lower back. Braxton, he saw through the hazy red film in his eyes, was nearly on top of the Technical when he started dancing like some torture victim wired to a hotbox. But the wheels were still in one piece, miracle of miracles, bags holding steady, far as he could tell.

That had to be the mother of all good omens!

Inspired that the gods of covert war had seen fit to smile down on him, Harmon dredged up all the seething determination at his command, spun against the white-hot surge of pain, Uzi stuttering at the armed militant he'd somehow missed. He was sure he tagged the man when the sky chose that moment to drop a comet on his head and turn out the lights.

AKHMADAH AL-HAMQUADRA didn't want to die. His single greatest wish was to survive this night, live, if only to regret the treachery of the infidels.

There was no sense berating himself now for the decision to hold hands with the American devils, not when the Financier's limousine was a short running distance away, sitting there, unmolested by the devastating explosions, even as the heavens still rained wreckage across the smashed remains of other vehicles. He took it as a sign from God he was meant to live, after all.

Assault rifle sweeping the conflagration, he fisted the blood out of his right eye. Never mind how many gashes ripped in his scalp and face from the explosion inside the hut, he was still breathing, hastening on a hard arrow straight vector away from what sounded the most bitter source of fighting.

Only...

He sensed some presence out there, circling, closing in on him from the south, using wreckage, flames and smoke as cover, as the autofire ceased. Several bodies were strewed near the back end of the main hut, where some of the GIA fighters had come running, only to fall as if poleaxed by an invisible source of killing. There! Was that a shadow, darting behind another pall of roiling smoke to the south?

The Financier came out of nowhere, materializing, it seemed to al-Hamquadra, from between two flaming shells of Technicals to his deep right. The sight jolted him to a braking skid, forcing him to tear his stare away the dark and armed specter he would have sworn he'd seen again a second ago. The surviving bodyguard, he saw, had his boss by the elbow, practically dragging him along, a crimson stain blossoming over the Saudi's stomach.

Briefly, he considered his options, sliding ahead, his weapon raking the blazing walls and drifting black smoke that seemed to expand a thickening ring around the motor pool. If he shot the Financier and his man, then there could be no report on his role in this disaster. As indirect as it was, he would still be held accountable by other power brokers for allowing the hated enemies of Islam to participate in the operation to begin with. Then again, if he helped the man flee— certain he could find medical assistance from one of several GIA camps backed by corrupt Algerian authorities in the vicinity—he would be a savior to jihad.

A hero, no less, lauded yet more for his courage under fire. Surely, more cash would thus be infused into his hands. The murderous fiasco here, the loss of so many fighters, the death of the State Department man could be explained away in due course...

There!

It was an armed specter, after all! Then he heard the bodyguard shouting his name to get over there and help, al-Hamquadra swinging his assault rifle around when the projectile streaked out of the smoky curtain. He hit the trigger, cursing the fact he knew he was already a fraction of a heartbeat too slow, the armed shadow vanishing like a ghost from his sight. He glimpsed the Financier and his bodyguard jerking as they were hammered by another invisible source of weapons fire a nanosecond before the explosion roared in his ears from behind.

Suddenly he was sailing through the air, his screams carried on the scorching fire and shock waves that were consuming him.

The crackle of hungry flames slowly parted the roaring in his ears, as he drifted up from several long moments of semi-consciousness. He found himself on his stomach, blood burning into his eyes. Spitting out the gummy strands, a sense of panic enveloped al-Hamquadra. He sensed the menace again, his hands scrabbling through dirt and rock. Where was his weapon? The militant groaned, winced. So much pain, all fire and twisting knives, in his back and legs, and with the slightest movement, it was all he could manage to look to the side, aware of the presence.

The fumes of burning gas, noxious smoke that carried the stink of blood and body waste swarmed his nose, threatening to bring on the vomit and unconsciousness. Somehow he dragged himself another foot or so, then spotted the assault rifle. He reached out for the weapon, a noise like a faint whimper locked in his throat, as he saw the tall shadow sweep through the black tendrils of smoke to his side, closing in long swift strides. The weapon he recognized as an M-16 with fixed grenade launcher, but it was the big custom fighting knife. Why was it in this man's hand, and wielded with such threatening intent? Why didn't he say something? Why not just shoot him and get it over with? What was he waiting for?

Al-Hamquadra felt the scream build, but it became trapped in his chest, as he strained to look up, so racked by pain his arms didn't want to move. He saw the face, slowly materialize into full view, it seemed, set in stone and smeared with black greasepaint, as the last wisps of smoke vanished. Then he stared into those penetrating ice blue eyes, certain he'd seen them before. Where?

Yes, familiar, so familiar…and…

The silent scream of pure horror tore through his mind as he recalled.

"JUSTICE MAN! COME ON. I know you're out there!"

Harmon slumped against the side of the Technical, watching as blood dripped from the hand holding the Uzi and spattered the top bag. The scream came from the south, like some animal, he thought, getting slaughtered. Now, the sound of terror had seemed to hold life all its own, suspended in the vile air of death. He listened to the consuming fires, eyes stung as he hacked his way through a pall of black smoke that seemed to sweep over the Technical, gusted in his face, as if by magic.

"Crusader! We can work something out!" A delayed explosion belched from the deep east edge of destruction. "Answer me!"

Harmon extended the Uzi, fanned the wall of flames, the smoke thinning enough he could scour the killing ground with some degree of decent perception. One, then two fiery sheets floated to earth, the double banging a noise like cannon fire in his punished senses.

He didn't need to call out to his men, or to the militants.

He was alone, and in the presence of Death.

Harmon started to feel the blood loss next, legs growing heavy, knees wilting like melting rubber. The world on fire rolled at him in misty waves. He needed help, and quick. His lower back had been shot through and through, two or three slugs taking something vital with them, he could be sure. Kidney, a chunk of liver…

"There's twelve mil, here. Justice man! We can split it!"

No answer. Was the bastard even still among the living?

Harmon opened the door, fell in behind the wheel. He was reaching for the key when he felt Cooper roll up to the side, thought he spied something long and steely winking firelight. He chuckled, why he wasn't sure. "I'm hit, big man. I need to get to our plane."

"You're not going to make it, Harmon."

"How come I was afraid you were going to say that? And after all we've been through together..."

Harmon swept the Uzi around, thought for one instant he could bring the bastard on-line, then heard the autofire.

"I ONLY SIGNED ON for a little loose change! I didn't know that crazy Harmon was looking to waylay you out here!"

Bolan kept the M-16 trained on the back of the pilot's head. The transport plane was rumbling down a narrow but flat dirt track, what passed for the closest thing to a runway in this area of desolation, as he was sure Harmon had already designated the stretch for evac. Unmolested flight on the way out wasn't guaranteed, as Bolan searched the vast empty blackness, the pilot running with lights out. Harmon had alluded on the way in that any MiGs were either grounded, or would steer clear of his arranged corridor over Algerian airspace. More shadow greasing.

"You kill Harmon and the other Killer Bees?"

Bolan didn't answer. He was whipped, more damage inside than to the flesh, it seemed, but there was unfinished butcher's work.

As soon as they put some miles behind them, Bolan would call Brognola.

"You might want to buckle up."

Bolan took the pilot's suggestion, settled into the copilot seat and strapped himself in. The soldier caught a whiff of himself. He reeked, like death. All the grime and ugly filth and vile odors that now clung to him from walking out the other side of yet another Hell on Earth. For a moment, he felt the ghosts of this one, a heavy grim burden on his soul, and all the way back to the hotel where it started. At this stage in his War Everlasting he shouldn't be shocked by the evil that men were capable of committing. But each and every time he saw and fought it now, the longer he stayed on the planet, he couldn't help but feel the grief and anguish burn deeper and harder through every fiber of his being. All the wasted life, he thought, especially, first and foremost, the innocent who fell by the hand of evil. It made him wonder.

Had he chosen his War Everlasting, or had it chosen him?

As for the wicked? He was perhaps pondering the obvious, but it was out of his hands once he finished making sure they couldn't contaminate, devour, thrive. Clearly, if the cannibals didn't desire anything but their own greed, bloodlust, power, pleasure and whatever else kept them rampaging through the innocent, the meek, the peaceful, then why would the wicked care about where their souls ended up? Or any other soul, in that regard.

The pilot's nerves began to show, eyes flickering all across the cockpit window. "You're not big on conversation, are you? Look, we're going to be in the air about—"

Bolan laid a cold eye on the man. "I'll tell you when to talk. Shut up and fly the plane." He looked over his shoulder. Banner was still wedged in the doorway. Beyond the look of utter defeat on the Killer Bee's face, Bolan read something else. There was greed, sure, as the soldier caught him glancing in the fuselage at the money bags.

And there was cold fear, shadowing the man's face next as the Executioner could well guess at what his stare was aimed.

They went wheels up. Stars above, in his eyes, but Bolan reckoned heaven was nowhere in sight.

Or did he have his own guardian angel? What would be his own accounting someday? If he was falling short somehow, if he was lacking...

Well, he was only human, after all. Some divine hand may or may not be on his shoulder, steering, protecting him as he waded into the next nest of human vipers to dispense Justice, to eradicate evil that had freely made its call to join the damned, thus sealed its fate in its own blood and shame. For now, he decided, let that be enough, let action settle all accounts, one way or another.

Spain was a few short hours away.

With luck, and the big Fed smoothing the way with intel and muscle that may need flexing to break down red tape walls...

Well, the Executioner might be able to catch Dragovan Vikholic just as the war criminal turned crime boss was waking up to greet the new day.

"MARTINA?"

His eyes flew open. There was something wrong, some presence in the room. A moment ago, he had felt it, heard something, but his senses couldn't sort out the noise, whatever the movement he'd just felt beside him. He called her name again, could feel her body next to him beneath the sheets, utterly still.

Dragovan Vikholic lay motionless, terrified to move a muscle. The world floated to him through hazy web of the high he'd been sleeping off, mouth dry, hair pasted with sweat to pillow. He was sick to his stomach, muscles aching, but he understood, accepted the reasons for the nausea and cramps. He needed another shot, if only to heave his bulk out of bed. A part of him wanted to detest his sudden fondness for the heroin he sold, but without it...

These days it was the only way he could fall asleep. No—it was the only way to sleep without the nightmares, raptured by the boneless sensation of floating outside his body, the warm euphoric peace the heroin spread through him, the only way he could forget the past. And even then, those living horrors came howling at him in the blackness of sleep. Despite all the booze and heroin and Viagra-fueled mad sex needed to drain his body and sweep away the terror the past would catch up to him. And when he awoke, like now…

He still saw, heard, "felt" them, living specters. Burned beyond recognition, the whites of their eyes staring from inside the smoke and fire, his name being chanted like a vile obscenity by legions of these things. He knew some of them by name, victims he had tossed into the furnace by his own hand, or tortured in ways they recounted, but in some incomprehensible peaceful manner that betrayed acceptance of their fate, and where they called to him from a place of bliss that some force surrounding them warned him he would never…

Then he would see the tiniest of bodies crawling out of the flames, sliding over the edges of the ovens.

Was he going insane? Was it the heroin? The booze? Was it the past coming to corner him, demanding justice? Simple as paranoia, the craving to survive, at any cost?

He stared at the ceiling, terror enveloping him like a living force of pure anger ready to rip him, limb from limb. Shadows seemed to dance across the room, expanding his dread of reality, then he recalled how the thunderstorm had knocked out the area's electricity, one of his men informing him that lightning had reduced their own generator to smoking trash beyond repair.

Candles. Dozens of them, in their stands, were posted like sentinels about the room.

He always needed some source of light these days, especially when he slept with the demons of his dreams. There had to be light when he came to!

He was thinking about the powder and the syringe beside the bed, body and mind screaming on the verge of withdrawal, when he saw something sliding along in the deep corner of the bedroom.

"Who's there?"

That sound of fear, how he hated what he heard in his voice, as it drifted across the room, hanging, then dying unanswered. It sounded so small, yet haunting.

He needed a gun in the bed with them at all times. Trust no one, least of all the CIA operatives who were supposed to be protecting him. Everyman was his enemy.

He rolled over on his side, arm reaching out, and nearly screamed when he looked into Martina's blank stare. He felt hypnotized by the red hole in the middle of her forehead, blood still trickling...

Vikholic found the Makarov pistol still clutched in her hand. Had she been roused suddenly from sleep by an intruder? Terrified thus, had she attempted to shoot but killed herself instead? Where was all his vaunted security?

He pried the gun from her grasp, threw the sheet aside, his breathing heavy, rasping in his ears. Hauling himself over the edge of the bed, standing, he fanned the room with the pistol.

"Nikimko! Radic!"

He was halfway across the room, wondering why nobody answered when thunder erupted above the roof. Crying out, he turned toward the curtained window, terror edging toward panic. It was only the lightning, jagged shadows streaked against the curtain. With each angry burst of thunder he flinched, then his wandering stare settled on the nylon bag near the dresser. There was their five million dollars U.S. in the bag, waiting for...

Why did it seem to have been moved? Why was it settled on the dresser? Or was this simply more paranoia, terrified imaginings?

He shouted for his men, the two operatives Harmon had left behind. Cursing, he turned, stumbling on, weapon raking the candles. The room was large, with couches, desk, bar, the corner pockets of shadow deep enough that light barely dented the darkness, where an armed intruder could be lurking.

He felt his finger tightening on the trigger, then he backed into the dresser, grunted as the sharp edge dug into his ribs. He was going mad, he decided, as those voices of his victims seemed amplified, hurtled at him by another ripped bolt of lightning.

He pivoted toward the bag, but sensed some new horror waiting for him, as he peered over the top.

Vikholic cried out, swept the bag to the floor. It took what felt like an hour for him to realize what stared him back. Acid sludge billowed up his chest, his mind screaming that the shadows were playing tricks on his eyes, but he couldn't deny what he saw.

Two severed heads had been dumped on the dresser. Harmon, he recognized, but it took another few seconds of combing his memory to know the head of al-Hamquadra had been brought back, as demanded.

Which meant if Harmon was dead...

Vikholic jumped as more lightning ripped from the skies, but sounded now as if it wanted to blast through the very roof above him. Trembling, he looked up, became slowly aware next he was staring beyond his own reflection in the mirror—

And saw the living ghost.

The face was framed clearly for an instant against another flash of lightning. The haunting chorus faded, as Vikholic wheeled, the curse rising in his throat, his weapon sweeping around to bear on the tall shadow he recognized. There was thunder and lightning, then a powerful blow to the head, before he spiraled into the dark.

# Epilogue

It was the morning of the third day after the night he now knew had changed his life forever.

He wasn't sure what exactly had possessed him to follow through to come here, but Andres Gadiz stopped on the hill and stared into the valley. The hamlet was pretty much as he remembered it, small stone dwellings, cobbled streets, the church rising at far north end, battered and weathered, having seen better days, long, long ago. The wooded hills were still dotted with their tiny homes, and he knew without having to look where he was going. Yes, it was a far cry from where he had called home in Barcelona for so long. But this poor, obscure and forgotten place, where he'd turned his back and walked off…

Was he really a new, a changed man? Only time would tell. Time was either friend or foe, depending on the individual.

The quarter million in U.S. dollars was maybe a start, the cashier's check sent anonymously to the church of San Juan by courier. There was a brief note attached that it was a donation in memory of Father Jose Gadiz. He was not looking to buy back his soul—only a fool would believe that, he knew—but he felt a need still for some visible sign of this sudden onslaught for atonement. That he didn't feel the first inclination to make known the generosity was a hopeful sign by itself.

The second act of reparation perhaps waited on the other side of town.

He felt another weeping jag threatening to overtake him, found it incredible, as exhausted as he was, that he still had tears to shed. For his brother. For Isadora.

For the wretched excess of countless transgressions that had caused so much suffering...

But the life he'd known—if he could even call it that any longer—had believed he had so cherished and so chased, no longer existed. Selling his share of the restaurant and the club to his partner had been the last act of letting it all go.

Ashes and dust.

Another time, another man, another soul.

Whatever his brother's ultimate sacrifice meant in the long run remained to be seen. He was, however, certain his brother's warning, coming at the price of his life, was all but clear.

There were only so many outrages one man could hurl at Heaven.

Andres Gadiz took the next few steps toward home.

THE SMALL PRIVATE VILLA on the beach was well north of Barcelona, but the madness and all its ghosts still haunted Bolan.

He was leaning on the balcony rail, staring out to sea, sipping on a beer. The soldier wasn't sure how he felt about the downtime now, granted him after his long conversation with Brognola, and following his silent smashing of the safehouse of Vikholic and his four-man force. He was grateful to be alive, no question, but torn between a range of emotions, from anger to relief to a sense of morbid wonder.

More than three days has passed, several lifetimes it seemed, since he'd touched Spanish soil again. One day alone had been consumed just sifting through the wreckage with the big Fed, then tracking down Katerina Muscovky through the American Embassy, a back and forth that had finally led the woman here. Safe and sound, but changed, he knew, by the entire experience. There was horror and relief at the same time, and he could tell she viewed him vastly different than when they'd met. Whether that was good or bad…

She was sleeping late at the moment, and Bolan couldn't blame her if she stayed in bed the rest of the day, all things considered. Whatever the rest of their time together…

He listened to gentle lap of waves, the screech of gulls.

There was still a hefty bag of questions left opened, and the soldier knew American and Spanish authorities were scrambling and scratching and bickering. It was a mess, to understate the entire shocking nightmare. The good news was that Bolan was nothing more than a ghost, as far as the politics, the SIU and Delta Force were concerned. Then there was the money, five bags already handed over to Brognola's agents earlier.

He recalled the fleeting anger he had felt a little while ago when watching the news, broadcast from the States via the satellite dish that came with the villa presented. It was sick in some way he couldn't quite define, but the news back home seemed more compelled to report on the tragic quadruple murders in Beverly Hills than the mounting body count in Barcelona. Apparently Bret Cameron had flipped out, shot to death his agent, Sid Morheim, a producer of some major film company that escaped Bolan and two female companions. Police found the star at some point later, slumped in a living room recliner, apparently dead from a drug overdose. It fit, he took the easy way out. As for the others who had lived through the terror alongside him in the suite, Bolan couldn't say. Somehow, he hoped, they would go on with their lives, altered and seared by the nightmare as they were.

They had to.

Tomorrow would come, he thought, as he heard the sliding glass door open behind him. He turned and found her standing in the door. There was something real and very human about the way she smiled at him, warm, decent.

He was grateful to be among the living, glad she was there.

Bolan returned the smile. When his time here was up, he would be back in the trenches.

There would be another Harmon, another al-Hamquadra.

His War Everlasting didn't rest.

# JAMES AXLER

# DEATH LANDS®

## Shatter Zone

In this raw, brutal world ruled by the strongest and the most vicious, an unseen player is manipulating Ryan and his band, luring him across an unseen battle line drawn in the dust outside Tucson, Arizona. Here a local barony becomes the staging ground for a battle unlike any other, against a foe whose ties to preDark society present a new and incalculable threat to a fragile world. Ryan Cawdor is the only man living who stands between this adversary's glory…and the prize he seeks.

### *Available September 2006 wherever you buy books.*

# TAKE 'EM FREE

## 2 action-packed novels plus a mystery bonus

## NO RISK
### NO OBLIGATION TO BUY